JACKIE CARREIRA
musician, and co-founder of Quirkhouse Theatre Company with her husband, actor AJ Deane.

Born in England to Portuguese parents, she grew up and went to school in East London, but also spent part of her early childhood in the Old Quarter of Lisbon with her grandparents. These colourfully diverse cities, and her 'genetic nomad' background, have always had a big influence on both her writing and her general view of the world.

Jackie now lives in Suffolk with her husband, two cats, and a ridiculous number of books, most of which she hasn't got around to reading yet. She spends a lot of time in public libraries, where there are even more books, but at least she doesn't have to dust those. She is a proud patron of Halesworth Library in Suffolk.

Since early childhood, Jackie has asked an awful lot of questions. Some people love it, some people hate it. It's probably about fifty-fifty. When she grows up she would like to be a philosopher and get paid to ask questions all day. Occasionally she would like to get some answers, but only if they are true.

More information and up-to-date news can be found on the website below, but it's much better just to switch off the internet and read her books or watch her plays.

Suffolk 2024

www.jackiecarreira.co.uk

For Laura,

Notebook Number Nine

Thank you for reading,

Jackie

Jackie Carreira

Troubador Publishing Ltd
Unit E2 Airfield Business Park,
Harrison Road, Market Harborough,
Leicestershire LE16 7UL
Tel: 0116 279 2299
Email: books@troubador.co.uk
Web: www.troubador.co.uk

ISBN 978 1 805145 14 1

British Library Cataloguing in Publication Data.
A catalogue record for this book is available from the British Library.

Printed and bound in Great Britain by CMP UK
Typeset in 11pt Minion Pro by Troubador Publishing Ltd, Leicester, UK

DEDICATION...

This book would not have been written if it wasn't for three particular people. To name them is not important, either to them or to you, dear reader. They will never know how much they inspired me to always try to be myself, but it seems that's all they've ever wanted for anyone they've ever met. This is an extremely rare quality in the world. I will try and do justice to that and look for ways to inspire others to be themselves, if I can, and whatever that might mean. I am part of their story as they will always be part of mine.

"The universe is a big place, perhaps the biggest."
(Kurt Vonnegut)

"Sometimes the questions are complicated and the answers are simple."
(Dr Seuss)

A very brief foreword

On the fourteenth of July in the year two-thousand, a powerful solar flare caused a severe geomagnetic storm on Earth that lasted for two whole days. This was later named the *Bastille Day Event* because it happened on the national day of France. The storm caused damage to GPS systems and power companies across the globe, and auroras were visible as far south as Texas in the United States.

Our story happens to begin on that very same day, but it has absolutely nothing to do with solar flares or what they might cause on our planet or anywhere else in the solar system.

Honestly, it's just a coincidence.

Incidentally, the year two-thousand was designated by the United Nations as the *International Year for The Culture Of Peace.* That would be a good idea.

Chapter 1

There was no clap of thunder, no ominous cloud, no catastrophic storm on the day that Notebook Number One began. It was actually quite the opposite, at least meteorologically. At the time, Bekki was sat in a stranger's garden at a faux-Parisian-probably-from-Homebase café table. A rich summer breeze blew butterflies and other erratic insects past the table as the sun picked out the colours of their wings in flight. Bekki only noticed them when they got stuck in her hair. Everything else receded into a July-coloured English country backdrop as she sat huddled over pen and paper in the neatly overgrown garden.

It was a pretty little garden in the heart of the Suffolk countryside. The owners of this particular holiday cottage had decorated the cosy interior with glossy-magazine charm in the fashion of the day - all ceramic floor tiles, low-slung ceiling lights, and feature walls of gigantic floral patterns on wallpaper. The online picture of the garden had been enough to entice Bekki to book it for a break away from the city. There was no garden back home. She sat on a driftwood bench at the table, just behind the Moon Gate and to the right of the laughing Buddha water feature. In this peaceful setting, so different from her flat-pack flat in North London, Bekki had an epiphany. She sat hunched over the notebook, sucking deeply on a Marlboro Light cigarette while trying frantically to write down what the hell was happening to her as it all unravelled in her mind. It was the year two-thousand. The dawning of a new era. This is what she wrote:

> *Lies! It's all been a massive bunch of lies! All of it! At least all of it that has been fed to me; to us, to you. To you? Who are you? Who the hell are you writing to, girl?? Okay, to ME. Write to me… Alright, I will!*

The furious scribbling carried on like that for another couple of paragraphs before any kind of coherence emerged. The rest of this missive was copied out later in the first of the nine notebooks – A4, both sides – seven of which are currently piled up on Bekki's bookshelves; the bookshelves that hold the old dictionary and the volumes of facts and figures and world statistics that were hardly opened anymore. Oh, and three or four works of fiction that just couldn't be thrown away for long-forgotten reasons. This is what the main section of the first letter at the beginning of Notebook Number One says, after the ranting of the first couple of paragraphs:

> *Dear Rebecca – or can I call you Alice?…*

But even before that, some explanation is required. Rebecca's name was given to her by her parents when she was just a few hours old, twenty-eight years before she booked that fateful weekend break in the holiday cottage in Suffolk. More precisely, her name was chosen by her mother, whose favourite book was *Rebecca* by Daphne du Maurier. She bought a highly-decorated, hardback copy of it for Rebecca's thirteenth birthday and the young girl read it in three days. She wasn't sure how to take the fact that it was the forename for the rather limp character in the book. The heroine seemed a bit needy with a rather glaring victim complex for Rebecca's liking. In any case, she resented the idea that the name simply wasn't hers. It was her mother's idea of a good name, probably because she herself had wished it was hers. Mrs Reeves always hated the name her own mother had chosen for her - Pamela. As a consequence, Rebecca's mother always looked as if she got more pleasure from saying the name out loud than her daughter ever did, which just didn't seem right to an adolescent searching for her own identity. Rebecca had sworn that, if she ever had a daughter, she would choose a cool name for her, which is probably what her mother and grandmother both swore. For another thing, Rebecca always thought that Du Maurier's book was a little overrated, but that could have just been her own budding insecurity masked by a healthy slice of stubbornness.

Rebecca's sister got off more lightly. She was called Jane after her mother's second-favourite book, *Jane Eyre* by Charlotte Bronte. A much more satisfying heroine to be named after, although a little too dependent on a man in the end, but I guess they were the times the novelist was living in. Her brother got off even more lightly. He was called Jimmy, *not* James, after her dad's favourite snooker player, Jimmy 'The Whirlwind' White. Obviously, he had been in charge of boys' names and his wife in charge of girls'. Not so romantic for Jimmy, perhaps, but always worth mentioning during pool tournaments down the pub. Especially when he was winning, which he did a lot. In any case, he wouldn't recognise romance if it dressed in black, swam a moat, and delivered a box of chocolates.

Bearing all this in mind, at the age of thirteen and three days Rebecca insisted, thenceforth, on being called Bekki with a double 'k' and adjusted her still evolving signature to suit. It started off as Bekkki with three 'k's', but she realised that was pushing the point a bit too hard, not to mention the racist undertones of having a name with 'kkk' in the middle of it, as Jimmy enjoyed pointing out to her very loudly and in front of his friends. So, Bekki with a double 'k' it would be.

From the first day that she publicly printed her new name - Bekki Reeves - on a piece of artwork to be hung in the school corridor outside the girls' toilets, she hated it, but she was far too obstinate at that age to take it back or to admit that she'd been hasty. Bekki and Reeves just didn't sound right together. It didn't flow from the tongue like Rebecca Reeves with that pleasing alliteration, but she'd stuck herself to it and couldn't budge without losing face. Her mother laughed. Her father shrugged. Her brother mocked. Her sister had no idea what was going on because she was only four years old at the time, but there it was. The name followed her around like an ugly blind date until she was twenty-eight years old. Until, that is, she wrote that first letter in Notebook Number One.

Let's go back to that July day, and that same afternoon when the notebooks were born. And thus, it began:

Dear Rebecca – or can I call you Alice?...

But before I copy out the rest of that life-changing first entry, perhaps I should explain where Alice comes in, because you might be wondering who the hell she is, as you probably should. When that first veil was lifted at the age of twenty-eight, Bekki realised, with no little trepidation, that she would have to start everything again from scratch. She would have to take everything she'd been told so far, everything she'd learnt by heart, everything she'd accepted, and replace it with something else that wouldn't make her feel sick to her stomach. But let's not give away too much too soon.

So, it occurred to Bekki, with the subtlety of a gas bill, that she would have to go right back to the beginning. It also occurred to her that brand-new things need a brand-new name so that we can recognise them and place them in context, and hang things on them in order to find them again in the future. That was very perceptive of her, so early on in the proceedings.

Choosing a new name for a new life was easy for Bekki. She would be called Alice – the character from *her* favourite book rather than someone else's. *Alice Through The Looking Glass*, that would be her. Now that all the preliminary explanations have been made we can start all over again:

Dear Rebecca – or can I call you Alice?...

One more thing before we continue. Of course, nobody else called her Alice. Not at first, anyway. Alice would have to remain a secret until she could stand on her own two feet. It's like giving birth to a child; not that she'd actually done that, but she had seen online videos and found them utterly gross. For the first few years, children need complete protection provided for them by their parents or guardians, at least those who are able to offer adequate protection. That should be the natural way of things. Children need food and shelter and warmth and the best environment that the parents can manage, until they can look after themselves. Most parents try to do the very best they can with however little or however much they know – which is not always a great deal these days, if the tabloid press are to be believed. But they do their best, I'm pretty sure of that. Only a tiny proportion of parents actually hate their children. But that's another, more tragic story that would need a lot of other notebooks. Not to mention the support of a good therapist.

Both Bekki and Rebecca felt a strong urge to protect Alice from the outside world until she was strong enough to protect herself. And the outside world, as she discovered on that warm July afternoon, was a place that new things needed to be protected from until they could build an immune system strong enough to withstand the sicknesses that were everywhere Bekki looked. However, that's something that comes out in Notebook Number Two...or is it Number Three? In any case, it definitely didn't come up until after the first grey veil of deception was lifted. And that's where we were before all these explanations became necessary:

Dear Rebecca – or can I call you Alice?
I am writing to you today because I don't know who else I can talk to. I don't know who else I can

trust. In fact, I am now sure that there's nobody else in the world that I can trust.

So, Alice was born on the fourteenth of July, twenty-four years ago at the age of twenty-eight. It wasn't ideal but that just happened to be the date of the first veil dropping away. Actually, if Bekki were going to start her life again she would rather have been born under the sign of Aquarius because they seem to have so much fun, but there it was. Alice would be Cancer the crab and have to learn to live with it. The fact that Rebecca was actually born under the sign of Gemini didn't even come into the picture. Poor Rebecca. Poor Bekki.

It took a couple of notebooks before Alice began to speak in terms of 'I' and 'me'. That's because Alice was born pretty much empty, as Rebecca once was, and it took a while before she felt it was possible to inhabit Alice to any great degree. I'm not saying that Bekki is Alice all the time, even now, but she certainly didn't want Rebecca to jump straight in there on that July day and soil the shiny new Alice with her hang-ups and complexes. That would have been too easy. She might as well have just changed her name by deed poll, then she would have chosen a surname to match: 'Alice Moonbeam? No. Alice Wonderglass? No, that's just silly. Alice Purethought? Ha! Definitely not. Too pretentious.' But I'm sure with time she could have come up with a good second name, maybe something with a hyphen, just for fun.

Or, when that first veil was lifted and her old, familiar world crashed down around her, she could have simply run away and disappeared forever. People do it all the

7

time. And she did think about it, but it didn't take long for her to realise that there was nowhere to go. When the solid, secure, heavy world that she'd always known suddenly became translucent and fragile, she discovered that it wasn't only like that in the garden where she was sitting. Oh no, it was everywhere. The whole damn world. There was no place left untouched by the deception that she had built her whole life around. So, in the words of Martha and The Vandellas, there was, in fact, *Nowhere to Run*. In any case, she only had one more night at the holiday cottage and, according to the cleaner, three chartered accountants from Cheam were due in by lunchtime.

Of course, Bekki could have chosen to get off the planet altogether in some dramatic, big statement kind of way, leaving behind only the first page of Notebook Number One and a swimming proficiency badge as her gift to the world. Firstly, that's not in her nature (thank goodness), and secondly, at that point she was still shit-scared of dying. She also had no idea where her swimming proficiency badge was, come to think of it. She hadn't seen it for years. She made a mental note to ask her mother about it the next time they spoke.

Consequently, Rebecca and Bekki decided there and then, the day Alice was born, to front it out. If nothing was actually how it had always seemed, then how was it in reality? What was behind the façade, if anything? She honestly didn't know at the time, and that's the truth. She only knows a little bit now, and the more she discovers the more she sees there is behind the discovery, and the less she knows in relation to all the new stuff she's just discovered there is to know. That sounds more confusing than it should be. Well, it makes sense to me and to Alice.

Most people only ask questions that they already know the answer to, or think that they do. They don't ask questions in order to learn something or to be corrected. They ask instead for confirmation of their own rightness, no matter how wrong it might be. And if they don't get that confirmation, they don't like it at all. Rebecca was not much different to most people, but Bekki was desperate. She began to ask questions because she was lost and had no idea what the hell to do or where the hell to go. Bekki put it best at the start of Notebook Number One.

On a further point of clarity: Bekki, who sometimes speaks as Rebecca, appears to talk to herself throughout most of the notebooks. On one level, this is perfectly true. There is a reason for this – she had nobody else to talk to, just like she said in that very first letter.

> *Dear Rebecca – or can I call you Alice?*
>
> *I am writing to you today because I don't know who else I can talk to. I don't know who else I can trust. In fact, I am now sure that there's nobody else in the world that I can trust. Nobody. Wow!*

The letter continues straight from this paragraph into the next one but in actual fact, there was a very, very long pause in between. The pause was so long that it was extremely uncomfortable for Bekki. There was no position that would accommodate it or provide any kind of relief; not sitting at the garden table, not standing with feet at a reasonable distance apart with weight evenly distributed, not walking around the garden sniffing the overgrown flower borders, not leaning on a fence of convenient height, not holding in your stomach while lifting your chest... you get the idea. It was very, very uncomfortable for Bekki. And it was as painful on the inside as it was on the outside. It was like waiting for someone important that you'd never met after leaving the house with your slippers on by mistake. Or being asked to speak in public when you've forgotten to change out of the 'No Shit Sherlock!' t-shirt that you save for slouching. There was a strong element of panic wrapped in a blanket of uncertainty. Too much was going on while at the same time everything was out of reach. The letter doesn't sound like that when it's read all in one go. For authenticity, there should have been a gap of maybe twenty blank pages, just to illustrate the void of understanding that existed. There was no clock in the garden to measure how long the pause actually was, but it must have been at least an hour. An excruciatingly long, slow, difficult hour.

In order to try and make some kind of mark about this, I've added five little dots to the copy of the letter here, all in a line on their own, just to remind us that it wasn't as fluent as the letter now reads in that first notebook:

Dear Rebecca – or can I call you Alice?

I am writing to you today because I don't know who else I can talk to. I don't know who else I can trust. In fact, I am now sure that there's nobody else in the world that I can trust. Nobody. Wow!

.....

Everything that I've come to rely upon as sturdy and familiar is just a sham. I don't know why I've never seen it before, perhaps it's easier not to. However, now that the veil has been lifted I can't pull it back down. That's what it's like, it's like everything has been covered with a curtain made of shiny surety and colourful permanence, but it's all been just a BIG, fat, ugly LIE.

I don't know where to start. You may think I'm being over-dramatic or exaggerating, but I'm not. If anything, I'm underplaying the horror of the whole thing.

Where do I start??

Well, for one thing, nobody seems to know why the hell we're all here! What's that all about? Or even worse, nobody knows where we're all going. Six billion humans, and counting, and we can't even agree on why we're all here. Shouldn't that be the first thing we're taught at school? Is that why children stop asking "why am I here?" at such a young age – because no-one will give them a reasonable answer? Are the Christians right? Or the Muslims? Or the Atheists or the Darwinists or the Jews or the Creationists or the bloody Jedi? Every single one of us is a human being that comes from the same place, yet we can't even agree on where that is. It's completely mad! Or is it all just random? That's even more mad! If it's all just random, why am I a human being and not a wasp-headed purple crane fly?...

At this stage in Notebook Number One, there are more and more examples given in a similar vein that become increasingly bizarre and gratuitously extreme, all to illustrate something that is actually quite simple. The point is really made at the beginning of that last paragraph, but we need to be a little forgiving and remember that it was still early days. Also, more than one large cup of filter coffee was drunk during the long pause mentioned earlier, and this had oiled the wheels of communication, as it were, and everything was just pouring out in one big, messy, caffeinated splurge with two sugars.

For the sake of accuracy from the start, it will be important for some readers to know that there were actually 6.07 billion human beings on the planet in the year two-thousand when our story begins. That, however, is a problem for other people's own notebooks.

After a couple more paragraphs, including a brief rant about advertising agencies and aerosol sprays that give your old Astra that 'new car' smell (actually, that bit was quite funny, but more on this subject later), the letter continues in a more reflective frame of mind:

Alice, I'm turning to you as my only hope out of the chaos and insanity of the world I find myself in. I am twenty-eight years old and I know nothing that is of any use towards my understanding of what it means to be alive.

It can't just be all about money and looks and cars and weight and jobs and children and popularity and everything else that has so far taken up ninety nine percent of my time and desire. What for? There must be some reason, some purpose to all this. Surely. Please say there is. I can't stand it if there isn't.

All these years I've been kept so busy with the ridiculousness of so-called 'modern' life that I feel like I've completely missed the point. I have no idea what it's all for. And because I don't know my own mind, I've allowed everything else to come in and take possession of it. I'm full of it, and it's all completely useless.

You are brand new, Alice. You've got a chance to start again before it's too late. You've got all the space in you that I've lost in myself; a space that is not yet corrupted by the desire to possess the absurd that we're all offered every day – and it is absurd. TOTALLY.

I want to make a deal with you, Alice. Let's start from scratch. I'll tell you everything I know that's real and useful – shouldn't take me too long – as long as we can share everything we find from now on that's actually true. From today I will protect you from all the crap that I'm full of while I try to get rid of as much of it as I can, if you will keep safe all the new stuff that actually means something.

Have we got a deal?
Yours in search of freedom from the horror,
Bekki x

And that was the beginning of Notebook Number One. That was Bekki's first desperate letter to Alice.

I read it back now and it makes me feel a little wistful. It also makes me feel immensely grateful and full of

13

hope. All of these feelings continue, to varying degrees, throughout the notebooks. They're sad and hopeful all at the same time.

Of course, Bekki couldn't tell anybody else about this at the time. She was worried that they'd think she was some kind of crazy lady; a schizophrenic with a resurrection complex; a nutter in denial. Actually, she's not. She never was. And she did check. There are plenty of online quizzes where you can. But when all of this started she was Bekki and also Rebecca, but not all of her was either or both. There was enough of her left unblemished so that she could write that first letter in an attempt to reach Alice. In fact, a big part of Bekki and Rebecca will always be in Alice, and she wouldn't have it any other way. Even if that were possible.

And, of course, Bekki is Alice – but not all of her is Alice. Not yet. Perhaps she never will be totally Alice. Perhaps she'll turn out to be something else entirely. Who knows? We're not finished yet. Bekki was just trying her very best to do whatever it took to stop herself from being so desperately lost.

This was the first ripple caused by the dropping of the first veil into a very big pond. That may be a mixed metaphor, or maybe just a bad sentence, but reading that first letter again always gets me a little excited.

At number one in the UK singles chart on that day was *Breathless* by The Corrs. This, like everything else, must be seen as mere coincidence until proven otherwise. In this case, it really is merely a coincidence, although Bekki felt quite breathless herself when she wrote that first letter. Pretty song, though.

You may be wondering who is writing this. I am the narrator. My name is Rea. Alice asked me to look after the notebooks, with agreement from Rebecca and Bekki, because she thought it would be important to look back on them at some time in the future. That time happens to be now. It is the year two-thousand-and-twenty-four. Much has changed.

There are nine notebooks in all – A4, both sides – seven of which are piled up on the white bookcase; the bookcase that holds the old dictionary and the volumes of facts and figures and world statistics that were hardly opened anymore. Oh, and three or four works of fiction that nobody could bear to throw away for long-forgotten reasons. Notebook Number Eight does not belong to us anymore. That will be explained later on.

What you hold in your hands is Notebook Number Nine. It's the culmination and distillation of all the others with the best bits kept safe in one place, and a healthy amount left where it is in the other notebooks because it doesn't matter anymore. It's also the end of the first chapter. There is always another chapter.

Chapter 2

There had been clues on both sides that things were not as they seemed even before that fateful day in July. It seems cruel of the gods (whoever they are) to have given we human beings the ability to only understand things backwards while all the time we're meant to be going forwards. Mostly we're all kept so busy just trying to stand still that we don't have time to stop and glance back at the footsteps we've been leaving behind; the patterns that are forming up in our lives that today needs to sit on, and tomorrow... what are we creating for tomorrow?

Rebecca was always a curious child. I don't mean she was strange, I mean she was full of curiosity. Bekki remembered the feeling of it with fondness and, because she liked it, she always managed to keep enough of that curiosity alive to pass on to Alice, despite whatever might have happened to Rebecca in the past.

There's a memory written in one of the early notebooks of when Rebecca was ten years old and almost at the end of her primary school education. Bekki, Alice, and even Rebecca know that most teachers truly, honestly do their best to educate children, but they're often so tied up in knots with bureaucracy and inspections and paperwork and curriculums that their best is forced to conform to the lowest common denominator, set by whoever happens to be in charge of educational policy at the time.

The following is not meant to criticise or demean all teachers, although there are a few that deserve to be stripped of their degrees and forced to work in sweat shops that make narrow ruled exercise books by hand for forty-five pence an hour. That was a direct quote from Bekki in the notebook and not me. She can be harsh, but real education is scarce within the schooling system. Pretty much all of us come out only knowing how to be a basic economic unit for the benefit of whatever the government of the day chooses to spend its – or rather *our* – money on. But this comes up in greater detail in later notebooks.

Anyway, there was Rebecca; ten years old, in a class full of all kinds of children in a primary school in Inner London. Today parts of this area of London are called 'underprivileged' while other parts, sometimes only a Chelsea Tractor's length away, are called 'bohemian'. To Rebecca and her friends, it was called 'normal' because they had nothing else to compare it to. All children believe their upbringing is normal until they reach a certain age. It's only when they look back from adulthood that they start to compare and criticise and use whatever childhood they had to excuse all sorts of behaviour that they want to get away with. Savvy therapists continue to make a fortune from this.

Young primary school Rebecca knew nothing of politics or social economics, which is as it should be at the age of ten. She was sitting in the first lesson of a part of the curriculum that concerned evolution. A subject both compulsory and necessary for the education of children who would become suitably benign members of society. But Rebecca had a problem. Before this lesson, she had been fed a different story, a story that came up every Easter alongside the chocolate eggs, and at Christmas time, alongside the mince pies, and refreshed again during weddings and christenings and funerals, alongside the cake and mini quiches. Even her own teacher, standing at the front of the class discussing amoebas and pterodactyls and Neanderthal man with diagrams, had cast her as second angel in the nativity play only a few months earlier.

Rebecca, being very curious as previously stated, could not stop her hand from shooting up into the air before the lesson was over.

'Yes, Rebecca,' said the teacher, 'do you have a question?'

'Yes, Miss,' said Rebecca.

'Excellent,' said the teacher, and she really did mean it when she said that. 'What is it, dear?'

'Well, Miss, I just want to get it right. Did we come from Adam and Eve or did we come from the monkeys?'

The teacher began at first by trying to explain to Rebecca, and the rest of the class, that these were two very different subjects, and it was best to concentrate now on what they were doing in this lesson.

Rebecca said, 'but Miss...'

Then the teacher went on to say that it was a matter of science versus faith, and we should not persecute people for their faith however ignorant or naïve it might seem to us in the modern day.

Rebecca said, 'but Miss...'

The teacher then spoke more firmly of science and the need to be logical and reasonable while, on the other hand, respecting other people's beliefs because you can't prove it either way. And, in any case, it was important that we learn about evolution as part of our education if we wanted to do well in exams, because qualifications are vital and the curriculum said...

Rebecca was never one to give up easily. That was the kind of child she was and the kind of adult she is today. She said, 'but Miss, it can't be both, can it?'

Of course, Bekki knows now that it probably is both, but that comes up much later in the notebooks. Sorry, I jumped ahead of myself again.

At this point the teacher asked Rebecca, firmly and with undeniable authority, to sit down, be quiet, and stop disrupting the lesson. Muffled sniggers sprang up around the classroom. These were nipped in the bud with one sharp glare from the teacher's bespectacled eyes. Rebecca heard the scoffs clearly enough before they subsided. She sat down and placed her hands firmly in her lap so that they would not shoot up again of their own accord.

This early and quite public exchange had a devastating effect on ten-year-old Rebecca. The realisation dawned on her with sadness and confusion that nobody was prepared to answer her genuine questions. Could it be that they didn't know? Or did they know but were deliberately keeping it from her? Why would they do that? She decided that she would have to find the answers for herself. She had to know why she was here and how she, and everybody else, had got here.

She tried very hard at first, trawling through books

in the reference section of the school library, watching difficult documentaries on BBC2, and generally ferreting around in places that she shouldn't be in. Then puberty hit, Rebecca became Bekki, and she almost forgot about the questions completely for several years. There are times in one's life when hormones are more powerful than questions of existence, and for Bekki this time lasted straight through her teenage years and into her early twenties. In those days, it was less about finding out 'why am I here' and more about stopping anyone new from getting here via her own reproductive system.

Then, when the notebooks finally began to be written, Bekki thought that she would look for any other useful clues in the old boxes that her parents still had stashed away in the loft. She didn't tell them what she was doing, and it didn't seem too strange to them that their daughter would want to revisit her childhood. If anything, they were pleased to clear some space and gladly gave her a cardboard box marked *REBECCA'S STUFF* in black felt tip pen. They tried to get her to take her brother and sister's boxes too, but she had enough to do sorting out her own history.

There were the usual special things in there: a certificate for swimming twenty-five metres (no proficiency badge, though), a booklovers badge from the Brownies, a painting of a purple and yellow house with orange smoke coming from the chimney by Rebecca Reeves aged 6 (ripped around the corners where it had been taken down from a classroom wall), a mauve and white ribbon that brought back no significant memories whatsoever, miscellaneous school photographs, a still anonymous valentine's card from nineteen ninety three, and a once silver-coloured ring that had since turned black. Who the hell sent that valentine's card? The bunny with the heart-shaped bosom and the cryptic, if somewhat clichéd, message inside that read: *From your very secret admirer xxx.* Who was it? It was probably her dad trying to be kind. She thought she recognised his capital 'F'.

Near the bottom of the box was a small pile of papers, including a handwritten short story about a talking pigeon called Pelvin, several truly awful poems that only an angst-ridden adolescent could relate to, and a few pages stapled together with the title: *The Universe.*

She remembered this piece of writing straight away. The date at the bottom confirmed it. This was written by Rebecca the day after that first lesson on evolution. This must have been her first serious foray behind the veil, only Rebecca could not possibly have realised its importance at the time. Alice didn't have to start from scratch at the age of twenty-eight after all. Rebecca had started it for her at the age of ten. It's just that she forgot for a long time, what with all the hormones and everything.

Let's just make it clear before we continue: there's nothing wrong with hormones and sex and all that goes with it, in its rightful place. The trouble is that nobody can seem to agree where this place is and what it's all about. Therefore, the human race has ended up with taboos and guilt and political correctness until it's all so confusing that we need books and counsellors and DVDs just to try and make us feel normal about something natural, or anything else that gets us through the night, as it were. What a bloody mess – sometimes literally. Bekki did manage to

22

arrive at some sound and simple reasoning about all this by Notebook Number Four, but it took her a long time and several mistakes. You won't find it here. It's too simple for most people to believe.

At the age of ten Rebecca was still free from hormones and sex urges and relationships so she had the space in her mind to be able to write the following on paper carefully torn from a narrow-ruled school exercise book.

But before you see it, I need to show you something else. After Bekki found this early writing she copied it into Notebook Number One, very near the beginning. Just before it she included a note to Alice:

Dear Alice,

Maybe we don't have to start quite from scratch – what a relief! The following is a piece of writing by ten-year old Rebecca. I don't know how I could have forgotten about it for so long. This must have been our first genuine question of any importance, and I think we should keep asking it. Please can you keep this safe until we start to get some answers?

Thank you and I hope you enjoy it,
Bekki x

It was copied out in blue ink with great care and Alice has looked after this early piece of writing ever since. All the original spelling and grammar mistakes were corrected, although Rebecca's spelling was actually excellent for her age, but the main body of the text is just how it was originally written in that dog-eared old exercise book. Neither Rebecca nor Bekki have ever claimed that the science in the piece is entirely accurate, but here it is all the same.

THE UNIVERSE

The universe is big. REALLY big. It's bigger than the biggest thing you've ever imagined and then a bit more. And inside this huge massiveness is everything you've ever heard, felt, seen, invented, and then some more.

We live in one of the outer parts of the universe on a bluey-green ball called the Earth. This ball is so awesome that we never, ever need to go outside of it while we are alive because everything we need is here. That's why our bodies aren't designed to live on the moon or Mars because we don't really need to go there, unless we're very curious, and then we can invent a space suit that is actually made from things you find on the Earth.

The planet Earth feels like it's standing still but, in fact, it's spinning round and round very, very fast. You may wonder why we don't fly off sideways, but there's a perfectly logical explanation for this, which is very simple if you ask a science teacher to explain it to you.

On top of all this the Earth moves all the time around a big, hot, yellow ball called the Sun. If it wasn't for this Sun our planet would have no light or heat so the flowers and trees wouldn't grow and it would be dark all the time and we probably wouldn't know when to get up in the morning because clocks wouldn't have been invented (they are machines that measure days).

The Earth is not the only thing that goes around this Sun. There are other different coloured balls that look a bit like ours with names like Mercury, Jupiter, Mars and Saturn, and most of these have one or more little baby versions of planets called moons that go around them, just like we do. All of these planets are at different distances from the Sun, which is why none of them ever bump into each other when they move around. It's very clever.

There's still more. Around all this there are millions and billions of things even bigger and more powerful than our Sun called Stars. A lot of these have big suns and medium-sized planets and little moons moving around them too, and the whole lot is moving round and round and whizzing through space right now, and it's been doing this for a very long time since the universe went 'Bang!'

Nothing seems to be able to get off the universe because you can't find the end of it, so nothing ever really dies, it just changes shape or goes to another place. That goes for everything, whether we can see it or not, because everything is made of energy.

What I mean by things we can't see is this: the universe is full, otherwise there would be gaps and if there were gaps people and even planets would fall straight through, and they don't. You can look straight through a glass of water but the water isn't empty, it's full of atoms and gases and organisms and all kinds of stuff. In the same way, the sky is full and so is what they call 'space' *(although it's not really a SPACE because that's like a gap and we'd all fall through again).*

Scientists have told us that the universe is expanding – perhaps it's expanding because it's so full – and this is a very difficult thing to understand. The universe is infinite. That means that it goes on forever and ever, and I'm not sure how you can make something go on forever even more than it already does. This leads me to believe that I'm not clever enough to have invented this whole universe. I'm not even clever enough to invent one human being on the little ball called Earth. Some of the cleverest brains on the Earth have tried to invent human beings like the ones we've got now and failed, so they couldn't have invented the universe either. They're not even sure where ideas come from (I know, because I asked my uncle who is a doctor), so something else must have done it.

Now this is where we come to something really big. A lot of humans on this planet call this something else God, Jehovah, Allah, The Great Architect, and lots of other names. This means that they don't really know who invented this universe either because they can't agree on who it was, but they all agree it was someone important because all these names start with capital letters and we are not allowed to laugh at them or call them fake, even if we think they are. Perhaps science will find them or it or no-one one day and then everyone will stop arguing about it and agree.

All I know is that whatever it was that made

everything go bang, it must have wanted us to try
and find them or it, because if you're clever enough
to invent the universe then you're clever enough to
stop us little humans from asking questions about
you. But I'm asking – how did all of this get here? I
really want to know.

I keep asking about this, but nobody has told
me the answer yet. I will keep asking until someone
does.

Rebecca handed this in as part of the class project on evolution at the end of term. On the last page, in red ink, was her mark: '*6/10 needs more thought.*' Rebecca didn't agree with that assessment at the time, but the teacher was right. It all needed a lot more thought. It wasn't a bad start, though. The most important thing was that it *was* a start, and Bekki was grateful that Rebecca had put the essay into that box, and grateful that her parents were obsessive hoarders. It meant that Bekki was not on her own. In fact, she never had been and now she never will be.

On the next page of the notebook was the very first letter from Alice. This is the whole of it:

Dear Bekki,

Thank you for finding Rebecca's story of 'The
Universe' and sharing it with me. Now I can
remember it for all of us. Now we can all remember
to never stop asking questions.

With love,
Alice.

Chapter 3

At first the notebooks were written in almost every day, and often several times a day, sometimes by Bekki, occasionally by Rebecca, sometimes by both of them at once in a mixed-up outpouring of ideas and questions and emotions. After the first letter was written, Alice watched from a distance and made sure that nothing was lost until she could step in and write some things herself.

From the second day in the notebooks, and for the first couple of months, Bekki was pretty harsh towards everything around her. The whole reveal had come as a big shock to her and she did what most people do when some new, all-encompassing concept overwhelms them – she wanted to get rid of everything that she thought was nothing to do with it, and as quickly as possible. It was as if she were possessed with the notion of a new life that she could see opening up in front of her, so she took the initiative without considering the consequences. Of course, she understands now that it wasn't very wise to act so rashly, despite the fact that most of the things in Bekki's life at that point absolutely needed to be cut away. It's just the brutality of it that she later came to regret. It almost ruined everything because that kind of behaviour, those kind of impulsive decisions, are not always sustainable.

It's like when a person wakes up on New Years' day and is horrified when they step on to the bathroom scales to find that they've put on five pounds over Christmas. So, they go off to the nearest gym with a brand-new resolution to get fit and actually keep the weight off this time. And they really mean it, on the day. They sign up for twelve months, with all the extras and new tracksuits and gym shoes, full of good intentions and thoughts of a new wardrobe and attractive friends and a pay rise and all the other dreams that gym membership is sold on. Six months later, after only three visits to sweat all over the running machines and drink expensive water from plastic squeezy bottles, the gym membership card is stuck behind a take-away pizza menu and the phone number of a local mini-cab firm, and the new gym shoes are slowly growing mouldy in the dark corner of a cupboard. Then next year, after too many chocolate oranges and glasses of Prosecco, the whole sorry mess begins all over again while the owners of the gym hold the revolving door open with a welcoming smile and a free purple hand towel.

In the same way, Bekki was quick to jump in and claim her membership card for a whole new life. She wrote to Alice about it quite early on:

Dear Alice,

I see now that what we're trying to do is massive and very, very difficult. We're attempting to swim against a tsunami-sized tide while having to live inside the world we're trying to reject. I'm not sure how I can do both. I have to find out what is real and what is a lie, but so far there are so many more

*lies than truths and I feel like I'm standing in front
of a massive brick wall.*

*Sometimes I think I'm such a hypocrite to carry
on with life on the outside like nothing's changed,
while all the time everything inside me is screaming
because I can see that it's a big fat lie.*

*Is it all just too big to take on? How can I carry
on with my life as it has been without going crazy?
It's too late to pull the veil back down. Once you've
peeked behind it there's no way of going back without
driving yourself mad.*

*There has to be a way…doesn't there? Or should
that be 'isn't' there? You see, I'm confused about
everything!*

Bekki

Alice did not reply to this letter. It was too soon. In
those days, there was a lot of frustration for poor Bekki.
She suddenly felt like an alien in her own world. She felt
- mistakenly, as it turns out - like she was the only human
on earth who was beginning to see things for what they
really were. She was the little boy in *The Emperor's New
Clothes.*

Bekki did try to talk to a selected few among her friends
and family about how she was feeling, but they couldn't
understand because she didn't know how to explain it to
them. It kept coming out muddled. All Bekki could do
was talk increasingly loudly and more vehemently on the
subject, like when English people ask for directions in
foreign countries. Some of her kinder friends were patient.
They listened and nodded for as long as they could before

changing the subject to something more palatable. Others just laughed and distracted her with alcohol. She stopped trying to explain to her mother very quickly when she suggested that her daughter might be working too hard and perhaps she should go and see Doctor Foley.

Bekki didn't go to see Doctor Foley, or any other doctor. She also stopped accepting invitations from certain friends to go down the pub. Instead, two days after the conversation with her mother, she wrote a short letter in her notebook:

Dear Alice,

I know now what I have to do. It's not possible to live in two worlds at the same time. From now on it has to be all or nothing. The choice is obvious.

With renewed vigour,
Bekki

Still Alice did not respond. It was still too soon. Bekki hadn't got it quite right yet, but she would eventually get the idea. In any case, everyone deserves a second chance and she was still a novice in the foothills of enlightenment, for want of a less fancy phrase.

Against Alice's better judgement, Bekki acted on that last note almost immediately and with relish. In many ways, the result was the right one for the next part of Bekki's journey, but the means of getting there were a tad rushed to say the least.

The first thing Bekki did was to quit her job at the advertising agency. Then she dumped her boyfriend of twenty-three months, Jake. I use the word 'dumped' because that was pretty much what it was. But first we need to deal with advertising, and in order to deal with it safely, let's give it a chapter all on its own and hope it stays there.

Chapter 4

For most of her first twenty-eight years on earth, Bekki might have been described as a normal member of society. 'Normal' to mean a person who has been trained to be fully receptive to the autosuggestion of advertising and marketing in all its forms. 'Most of her twenty-eight years' meaning all but the time when she was a baby and hadn't yet learned to ask for things she'd seen on TV, movies, shop windows, billboards, magazines, and most recently on the ever-expanding internet. Toddler Rebecca did, of course, learn, as we all do.

The next entry in Notebook Number One was written in the form of a frenzied list. Reams of transcribed notes were scribbled down on various bits of paper - whatever she had to hand at the time - all glued down on to the pages of the notebook, one after the other, some crooked, some straight, to show a kind of progression. The information didn't really develop or evolve. It just sits there, to this day, like some kind of tombstone to Bekki's old life. It reads as if Bekki were frantically writing it all down superfast as it was coming at her. I guess Rebecca and Bekki had never noticed just how much had been coming *at* them all the time, every day, seven days a week. Writing it down made it seem more real. It was a purge, like those people who shove coffee up their posteriors to get rid of all the toxins in their bodies. I hope they wait for it to cool down first.

There were pages and pages of this stuff in that first notebook. It came out too fast for Bekki to catch it all, but I'll copy out just a little of it to give a flavour of the whole. I could have picked any page, they were all very similar. Bekki could have carried on writing it down for months. It was relentless. She realised that there wasn't any point in continuing after the first ten minutes but it must have given her a rush, which is ironic, really. Reproduced here is more than you need in order to get the picture.

THIS IS WHAT MY TV TOLD ME TODAY
(Saturday 5th August 2000)
20 channels in 10 minutes:

"I've fallen for the hype!... (*click!*) I used to think only luxury brands could give me beautiful hair... (*click!*) Will you take a moment to care about animals?... (*click!*) 'I just need to be free'... (*click!*) Straight on, full throttle, and he crosses the line in 46 seconds!... (*click!*) We'll also give you the window cleaning tool absolutely free... (*click!*) If you have a photo that you'd like us to show, why not send it in?... (*click!*) I've been told that my boobs are my best feature... (*click!*) If they were put on the market and the buyer gave them a good clean, then I would say, for insurance purposes, they'd would be worth between £4,000 and £6,000 for the pair... (*click!*) Don't just clean it – steam clean it! Yours for only 84.99... (*click!*) We'll even send you a bonus workout DVD... (*click!*) Can 32-year-old Amber

Tucker secure the $100,000 investment she needs for her new fast-food idea – Humongous Wieners?... (*click!*) I cuddle my children, so it's not my fault she's gotten into drugs... (*click!*) The incredible expanding hose! You will never be bothered by kinks again... (*click!*) Including your face, underarms and bikini area... (*click!*) It's the must-see movie of the year... (*click!*) The government have defended their changes to the welfare system... (*click!*) I couldn't pick them out in a line-up... (*click!*) From Afro-Caribbean right down to fair, this gives you that soft, flawless finish... (*click!*) They sentenced me to a total of 28 years in prison... (*click!*) You'll watch your body transform after only 20 minutes a day... (*click!*) You've got to be in it to win it... (*click!*) And that goal came straight down the middle, totally out of left field... (*click!*) A woman and an eight-year-old girl have died in a houseboat fire on the Norfolk Broads... (*click!*) North Korea have denied that they've just completed a new round of nuclear testing... (*click!*) And Granny's Tinker wins the Irish Grand National in a surprise result... (*click!*) Thick, smooth, and deliciously creamy... (*click!*) This is a battle for hearts and minds... (*click!*) Go on, indulge yourself... (*switch off*).

The number one single in the charts on that date was *7 Days* by Craig David. Bekki hadn't listened to Radio One or watched *Top of the Pops* that week. Nevertheless, the next seven days were as big for her as they were for Craig David, but in very different ways.

Bekki wrote a letter of resignation to her boss at the advertising agency on the following Monday. She didn't show it to Alice in advance, but she did paste a copy of it into the notebook afterwards. Later she thought better of it, tore it out, thought some more, and then pasted it back in again. It got a little torn in the process, but it's there for posterity.

Bekki's boss had an important breakfast meeting with a new client that morning, discussing market penetration for a new chain of fitness centres over chocolate croissants and cappuccinos. He didn't open Bekki's letter until eleven-thirty.

After two and a half hours of squirming in her ergonomic swivel chair, Bekki was called into the boss's office. This is the letter that he responded to: -

Dear Julian,

I wish to hand in my one month's notice as of today for the following reasons:

1) *I no longer feel that I can continue working in this industry with a clear conscience. Everything that we do has become abhorrent to me. The whole of the advertising world revolves around selling things to people who don't need them and/or can't afford them, and I just don't want to be a part of it anymore.*
2) *I now wish to use my time and energy usefully and productively in the pursuit of truth and the real purpose of life, and will look for employment in a field that is not contradictory to this.*

3) *I would encourage you to think likewise about your own position and search your conscience as I have done. If you wish to discuss this further with me, I would be happy to do so.*

As I cannot afford to be unemployed for too long, I would like to ask for time off (unpaid if absolutely necessary) to attend any job interviews that I can secure. I would also ask if you would be willing to provide me with a reference as I have been a good employee up until now.

Thank you for your understanding in this matter and I wish you well in the future.

Yours sincerely,

Bekki Reeves

Bekki regretted item number three in the letter, but only once she'd printed it, sealed it in an envelope and left it with Julian's secretary. That was an early lesson for Bekki: always leave important letters unsealed in a drawer for at least eight hours before re-reading, editing if necessary, and then sealing and sending. The same goes double for drunken text messages and late-night status updates on social media. But it was too late now. The deed was done.

Later that morning, Julian called Bekki on her direct line and asked if she would like to go to lunch with him at Café Bleu in Malcolm Street to discuss her letter. Julian only ever asked Bekki out to lunch with him twice during her time with the company. The first time was at the end of her starting week at the agency, in order to welcome her to the company and to show what a caring, thoughtful and mega-cool boss he was.

'I want you to think of me more as a friend than a boss,' he had said on that first Friday. 'I'm the kind of dude who sees this not just as a business but as a family; an adopted family who all share the same goals, if you will. If you need anything at all, just come and see your uncle Jules.' He laughed a little at his own joke as he said it. Bekki didn't know it was a joke. There was no clue because it wasn't funny.

That first lunch had continued for precisely an hour in pretty much the same vein. Julian did most of the talking in one long, polished advertisement with himself as the product; a commercial where Julian was the star, as snappy and heartfelt as any insurance company ad, which was his speciality, incidentally. Bekki bought it at that first lunch because advertising works on almost everybody almost all of the time. But then she was younger and more open to slickly delivered suggestions.

The second lunch was the day that Bekki had sent the resignation letter. How neat to finish the way it had begun. In between the two lunches Bekki had simply slotted into 'the family' like an overlooked middle child, never the first or the oldest with all the pride and promise that goes with it, and never the youngest with all the fuss and protection that goes with that. Meanwhile, Uncle Julian had stayed in his top floor office, regularly circulating encouraging emails to thank his 'family' for the copious amounts of cash that continued to swell the company bank accounts and pay his generous annual bonus.

Now, at five minutes to one, Bekki was waiting in

reception for her second and final lunch with the boss. Julian arrived at five minutes' past. Always keep them waiting long enough to get nervous, but not long enough to get angry. That's how he rolled. Malcolm Street was just a short walk from the office and Julian strode slightly ahead of Bekki in purposeful, linen-suited silence until they reached Café Bleu. A table, dripping red and white gingham, had been reserved by the window. Once lunch had been ordered and glasses of Merlot poured, Julian began as if there had been no previous awkwardness. The conversation went exactly like this:

'So, my dear, what's all this about you wanting to leave our mega-marvellous company?'

'Well, it's nothing personal against anybody, but...'

'I should hope not. You know, I've always thought of this company more like a family...'

'I know.'

'...and family means everything to me. So, you tell your uncle Jules where you think the problem is and we'll see if we can't fix it together, okay?'

'Okay.'

'Cool. And don't feel you have to keep anything from me because I'm a big dude with broad shoulders – and that's not just because of all the hours I spend in the gym, ha ha! No. So, you can be as free and as straight with me as you like, little sister. This is between you and me, and you've got my word on that. I want to help you, sweetie. You're an important part of the team.'

'Okay, I'll try.'

'Great! That's all I ever ask of anyone, that they try. Whatever the result, it doesn't matter as long as that person

41

tried their best. That's what I always say. As long as they've given it one hundred and one per cent, as long as they've sweated, as long as they've reached, I don't mind what the outcome is. And I really do mean that.'

'Yes, well I don't want to work in the advertising business anymore, however hard I try.'

'Right! Great! So now we can get at it. Tell me what's on your mind, honey.'

'I just don't believe in it anymore, and because of that…'

'Oh, Bekki, Bekki, Bekki. How old are you, my love?'

'Twenty-eight.'

'Twenty-eight. Good age. Do you know how long I've worked in the advertising game?'

'Twenty-one years.'

'Twenty-one years. That's nearly as long as you've been on this planet. Ha! Can't believe it's been that long. The years fly by faster and faster. God, that makes me… *(Julian counts on his fingers)* that makes me five years older than I actually am – Ha! But, do you know what? I wouldn't have changed a second of it. I've never stopped learning and I've never stopped getting better and better at what I do. That's what hard work does. And the excitement has never left me, you know. It's always been a buzz, and I'm a buzz junkie. Do you know what I say every time we secure a new account?'

'That's another human being saying: 'Thank you for being so awesome?'

'Right. That's another human being saying: 'Thank you for being so awesome!' And that's what's important. That's all that matters. This is a human business. We are in the business of making people's lives better. If it's better for one member of the human race, it's good enough for me, don't you think? I mean, what other industry can say that, huh?'

'Well, that's my problem...'

'Bekki, my dear, there's so much still for you to learn – and I know we can teach you. You never stop learning in this game. What else can you say that about? You learn from the best and you learn from the worst in equal measure, do you know that?'

'Yes, I do.'

'So, learn from me, sweetheart. Let me teach you.'

'That's just it. I want to learn about real stuff, not...'

'If I can interrupt you there, honey – let me share with you my philosophy of advertising. Think of this as a free masterclass...'

Bekki slumped slightly in her chair, picked up her fork and started on her deep-fried Camembert. Julian spoke right through the remainder of lunch. It was the same advertisement as four years ago, only this time in HD-ready, digital surround sound with three anorexic supermodels, one Hollywood A-list voiceover and a backing track by the Black Eyed Peas. Bekki worked her way through asparagus and broad bean risotto with truffle shavings, tarte au citron with blackcurrant coulis, two large glasses of Pinot Grigio, and a double espresso.

Uncle Julian walked Bekki back to the office, gave her a distinctly middle-aged high five, and then turned to collect his messages from Saffron on reception. Bekki went back to her office, packed her few possessions into a cardboard archive box and left a brand-new letter on her desk. She didn't keep it for eight hours in a drawer to re-read and edit it later, she just left it to be found where it was.

> *Dear Julian,*
>
> > *Thank you for taking me out to lunch today. The food was excellent. I hereby give one months' notice as of one month ago. I just don't fit in here anymore.*
> >
> > *Good luck,*
> >
> > *Bekki Reeves*

It was three-fifteen in the afternoon when Bekki left Pitch Perfect Promotions advertising agency. It was warm but cloudy with a hint of drizzle in the air. She never heard from her uncle Julian again. She didn't get a reference but later she did get a voucher for ten percent off gym membership from an old client and a free purple hand towel with the company logo on it.

At three-thirty-eight that same afternoon, Saffron found Bekki's letter and took it straight in to Julian. At three-forty-two, he wrote a memo and faxed it to all departments:

> *Hey Team!*
>
> > *I've been doing a bit of blue-sky thinking and come up with a parachute of an idea! More and more people are switching off TV ads, clearing computer cookies and looking for the 'truth.' Let's give it to 'em with both barrels!*
> >
> > *New campaign buzzwords: REAL. PURE. LIFE. LOVE. TRUTH, etc. etc. Ditch the glamour;*

pitch Babies, Fat People, Uglies, Holys, People in wheelchairs - you get my drift. The conscience dollar is gonna be HUGE!

Ideas?? On my desk by the end of the week. Best pitch gets a weekend in Amsterdam and a crate of Pinot.

Jules x

Later that evening, Bekki went to a second floor flat in Finchley to dump her boyfriend. She was on a roll.

Chapter 5

Jake was four years older than Bekki, but maturity has nothing to do with age. They had been in a relationship together for almost two years, which had slipped by with little incident. Overall, it had been a smooth and quite pleasant experience, including a fortnight's holiday to Valetta. No spikes, either high or low. That would be enough for most people in a relationship.

To begin with Bekki found Jake's boyishness rather attractive. She preferred to think of it as childlike and endearing and loved his lack of cynicism. A good sense of humour, which was on the wish list of every woman searching for a mate, according to every magazine survey that had ever asked, could be ticked on Jake's behalf too. He always found time for games of all kinds, and had a certain crude mental and physical dexterity because of this. Perhaps it was just good hand-eye coordination, nothing more, but Bekki had always given him the benefit of the doubt up until now, choosing to believe that it was wit rather than gamesmanship.

Jake was two inches taller than he looked, which is unusual as most people are actually shorter than they look, especially in photographs. The loss of Jake's natural height came from years of curling his upper body around pints of beer, joysticks, and remote controls. Mind you, if he had stood up to his full height people might have noticed that his legs were too short for his body, so the slight stoop actually made him look perfectly in proportion. It was as if he were built for his lifestyle rather than his lifestyle causing his build, which was, in fact, the case.

He had an indefinable kind of attractiveness, the sort of face that people call 'cute' after pausing when asked and without being able to point at exactly where the handsome bits are. The wrinkles at the corners of his eyes helped a lot because he always looked like he had just rested a tired smile across the top half of his face. His eyes were actually too small because it was impossible to tell whether they were blue or green unless you got really, really close and peered through the neat little gap between his eyelids. They were, in fact, a sort of muddy grey but his dark, curly eyelashes made them seem lighter by contrast.

It was impossible to know whether Jake's hair was curly or straight because he always kept it shaved so short that a person could only be certain of the sweep of the hairline. This was pencil straight on the right side of his face but distractingly bendy on the left. It was a quirk that Bekki used to find attractive, and then rather irritating.

The overall effect of Jake's appearance was that of a man slightly out of focus. It was as if you could see him and describe him but only with your head at an angle and your eyes slightly squinty. A person could tell that there was more to him than meets the eye but it was as if when you stared at one part of him, another part of him disappeared so that you could never look at the whole of him in one go, as if he were like a binary star in a night sky, or a Bruegel painting with tracksuits. All in all, he could be best described as 'not unattractive.'

Jake had a comfortable satisfaction extending from himself and a strange, unquestioning trust that reached out to everyone who spent time with him. He was a man's man, for sure - if the man in question wasn't too manly - but women found him a lovely combination: unchallenging while still worthy of taking on as a part-time project. This was mostly due to his casual, almost ignorant sense of style. It was obvious that his mother still bought most of his clothes. The rest of the items in his wardrobe were probably birthday, Valentine's or Christmas presents from ex-girlfriends plus a couple of t-shirts that had evidently been given to him free with multiple purchases of various products that he'd either eaten, watched, or used a lot of in the bathroom. This hadn't been a problem. Neither Bekki nor Rebecca had ever been accused of being a fashionista, something that had caused years of eye-rolling from Jane during disappointing shopping trips to Oxford Street.

Bekki had her own key to Jake's flat and had previously enjoyed the sense of security that she felt when letting herself in to her boyfriend's home. It showed he had nothing to hide from her. It made her feel like a special person in his life. She didn't know, however, that her key was one of seven which had been cut and circulated. Jake's mum had one (obviously), two ex-flatmates and a current one had three more, another was left with the couple downstairs in case of emergencies – although they'd been away travelling for six months and he couldn't remember what their names were – and ex-girlfriend, Katy, had the seventh. Katy had left Jake almost a year before he met Bekki because 'it just wasn't going anywhere' and he had forgotten that he'd given her a key. It didn't matter, though. She had no intention of ever coming back.

Tonight, for a change, Bekki felt a pang of guilt just casually letting herself in to someone else's home to break their heart, so she rang the bell instead. There was no answer so she rang it again and left her finger on the button a little longer. The silent pause once the bell stopped ringing was unexpected. The space it left in Bekki's mind was quickly filled by nervous doubts and unrequested feelings of hypocrisy because, as we know, nature abhors a vacuum. She didn't ring the bell a third time, but slowly, knowing it was for the last time, she slipped the key into the lock and let herself in. She called to Jake and he answered from the living room.

'It's me, Jake. Are you okay?'

'Hi. Yeah. I'm just finishing off this level... die, scum, die! Do you want to put the kettle on, Bekks?'

Bekki stood at the living room door with her jacket on for a moment. She watched Jake as he sat decapitating the digital undead from the luxury of his sofa. This was accompanied by impressively realistic sound effects, mostly of his own making. He looked so much younger than his years as he jabbed that button in delighted frenzy, young and happy like a little boy who's had the same pants on for four days because it's the school holidays. He was aware of her presence, but his mouth spoke in her general direction while his eyes stayed on the game.

'You alright, Bekks?'

'Not really.' Bekki hadn't moved from the living room

door. She wasn't sure whether just to blurt everything out and walk away, or put the kettle on.

'Aw, bad day at the office?' asked Jake, not expecting a long answer. 'I've nearly finished this level, then I'll be with you.'

Bekki decided to take the longer approach. 'I'll put the kettle on.'

The kitchen, as usual, was tidy because it was almost bare and hardly used. Jake wasn't really a kitchen person. Bekki put the kettle on and made two coffees. She made Jake's in his favourite *'I'm not sleeping I'm just moving really, really slowly'* mug with the sloth on the side, and waited until all the zombies on the current level were liquidated. She sat next to him on the sofa, took the joystick out of his hands and placed it on the arm of the sofa. Then she told Jake that she didn't want to go out with him anymore. She told him that she needed some time for herself to deeply consider where her life was going, what it was all for, and what she was going to do about the epiphany that she'd had on a long weekend in Suffolk. She didn't go into great detail, except to say that she needed to go on this journey alone.

Jake listened and then asked if it was anything he'd done. She said, 'No, it's not you it's me.' He knew then that it couldn't be him because it wasn't the first time that it hadn't been his fault but his girlfriend's problem. He was therefore relieved but more than a little sad at Bekki's answer. He asked a second question: 'Is there anything I can do to make you change your mind?' Bekki shook her head and looked down with a nervous kind of sadness at her hands resting in her lap.

Jake put his coffee cup down on arm of the sofa next to the joystick. He picked up Bekki's hand, lifted her chin so that he could look straight into her eyes, and wished her well for the future. After a final hug and a ceremonial placing of Bekki's key to Jake's flat on the hook in the kitchen, they said goodbye with a little sigh on both sides.

'Keep in touch, yeah?' said Jake.

'Sure,' said Bekki, although she wasn't sure of anything in that moment. She felt like she was bobbing in a sea of uncertainty, just off the coast of Insecurity Bay without a life jacket or packed lunch.

'If you need anything…' Jake began.

'I know where to find you,' Bekki finished.

'Take care, Bekks.'

The front door was closed gently behind her when Bekki left. She stood still for a moment and almost rang the doorbell again to say that she was wrong and could he just ignore the last half an hour, but she knew that was merely an understandable hiccup of fear. As she walked away down the street towards the bus stop, she could feel intensely that she was travelling into the unknown as a single woman approaching her thirties. For most people in their twenties, that's pretty scary. Almost all of them get over it, though. Ask anyone in their fifties.

Jake made himself another cup of coffee and a peanut butter sandwich and settled down to kill some more monsters. He found himself sighing unconsciously a few times through the next two levels. He liked Bekki a lot and he was sad, but he knew he would be okay in the end. He always was. Who knows, she might even realise that she had made a mistake and come back to him sometime in the future. And if she did come back, he decided that he would forgive her with no hard feelings. He missed her already.

Before the undead slaughter was done, Jake's flatmate came home. Howard was ten years older than Jake but really, really didn't want to be. He was divorced and had a hairline that was receding only slightly quicker than his chances of marrying again, but he was in denial about both of these things. However, Jake was pleased that Howard was home early so that he could nurse his newly-broken heart in the company of one of the guys.

'What's happening, my man?' asked Howard, dropping his keys with a clatter onto the little plastic table by the door.

'Not much,' replied Jake. 'Had a bit of a shit day, to be honest.'

Howard dumped his jacket on the floor next to the TV and tilted his head to one side in order to display fraternal sympathy to his flatmate. 'How so, bro?' This phrase sounded absurd coming out of his forty-two-year-old lips, but Jake didn't mind, mostly because that was the kind of forgiving guy he was. Also, he was used to it. That and other out of place phrases like 'Phat' and 'Fly' and 'Mo Fo,' which Howard pronounced as 'Muh Fuh,' much to the annoyance of all his mates except Jake. 'You wanna talk about it, man?'

Jake shrugged his shoulders, but he did want to talk about it. 'Bekki came round to the flat earlier tonight to dump me.'

'No way, dude! That's heavy shit, man. I thought you two were solid.'

'Yeah, so did I. Came out of left field, to be honest.'

Howard slumped down on the sofa next to Jake. He gave him a gentle punch on the arm to signify manly affection in a time of emotional crisis. 'Women, huh? Who knows what goes on in their tiny little minds.' Howard certainly didn't. 'You okay, bro?'

Jake nodded and retrieved the joystick from the arm of the sofa. 'I will be, I guess.'

'Sure, sure, course you will. What doesn't kill you, dude.' Howard didn't bother completing this particular platitude. He didn't really mean it either because he wasn't sure that he believed it. He thought it was just what you say in order to move a conversation on to the next bit.

'I liked her a lot, though, bro,' said Jake. Just then, his finger-tapping on the joystick increased as he aimed a series of knife throws at a particularly large and ugly creature on the screen.

'Her loss, dude,' said Howard. 'What level are you on?'

'Sixteen.'

'Cool.' The middle-aged hippy reached down behind the sofa to retrieve a vintage 1957 Martin acoustic guitar. This magnificent instrument was worn in all the right places by a succession of bedroom guitar heroes. It was a thing of beauty and the only thing Howard owned that was worth more than a tenner, including the entire contents of his wardrobe and chest of drawers combined. He gave the guitar a strum, made a small adjustment to the 'A' string machine head and strummed again. It was perfectly in tune. Its tone was like the breath of a husky angel. 'Hey, man,' said Howard, 'do you want me to teach you how to play the guitar tonight?'

'Yeah, if you like,' said Jake. 'I'll just get past this level first, then I'll go to the offie and grab us some beers.'

Howard nodded agreement and plucked at the strings. The opening notes of *Stairway to Heaven* flew like blackbirds out of the guitar. It was going to be a long night.

When Bekki got back to her flat she wrote a letter in Notebook Number One. She wrote it before she'd even made herself a cup of coffee or a peanut butter sandwich or checked if there was anything good on the telly. She didn't have any monsters to kill or instruments to learn how to play. She hadn't bought any beer on the way home either.

> *Dear Alice,*
>
> *What have I done? Jake wasn't a bad guy and he took it so well that it made me feel like a total rat. How can everything feel so wrong and so right at the same time? Am I just being stupid? Perhaps I'm just losing the plot. This is all ridiculous. Everything's changing and yet I feel like I've taken a massive step backwards. I'm not getting anywhere with this. And now I'm doing it all on my own. Maybe Jake would have understood if I'd given him a chance... No, wait. I'm just kidding myself. He probably wouldn't. Nobody does.*
>
> *Shit!*
> *Bekki x*

And then, just when Bekki was feeling totally alone, and before she could give up and finally check if there was anything good on the telly or pop down to the offie for some beers of her own, Alice responded...

Dear Bekki,

I see that you are in some difficulty and I want you to know that I'm here.

Stop for a moment. What's the rush? You ARE getting somewhere, not because you're in a hurry, but because you want to and you mean it. Try to use that feeling of wanting to get somewhere, not as an excuse for frustration, but instead as a battery store for patience.

Learn the art of waiting and make the best of the valuable time that it provides. It does not rob you of time (such a precious and short thing for human beings, as you will learn) but instead it makes a gift of it.

We were once asked to pass on some advice to our little godson, Louis, about Patience when he was having a bad time at school. Yes, it was 'we', because I helped you with it. You just didn't know that at the time. Do you remember what we said? It was brilliant, and it was this:

'Sometimes you have to wait for something you want, which calls for Patience, because not everything can be ready right when you want it to be. If you find this difficult, try doing something you love while you wait. Then, when it's ready, the thing you are waiting for will find you happy instead of angry, which is always better.'

That was the advice we gave to an eight-year-

*old child, and it's just as valid for you now. There are
so many things that you love to do; so many things
that make you smile. Use this time to do some of
those things instead of being frustrated at the lack
of time you have. It's a madness that only keeps you
stuck where you are.*

*GAIN WIT from WAITING and you might be
amazed at just how many of the things you ache for,
chase and grab for, were close by the whole time. It's
simply that they couldn't get near while you were
trying so hard to run at them head first.*

*You're not alone, Bekki. I'm waiting with you
and for you, and I know that you will be worth
waiting for.*

Alice

Bekki still had the pen in her hand the third time she
read that letter. She knew that her hand had written it, but
she was also sure that she hadn't, and nor had Rebecca.
It was strange but reassuring. For the first time, Bekki
realised that Alice wasn't a simple, empty, hopeful child
that was starting from scratch. She was way ahead of her.
This was somebody she could learn from. Where had she
been all her life?

Alice said she'd been waiting for them both, for Bekki
and Rebecca. She was telling them things they knew but
had never seen or recognised. She'd been watching and
listening all this time. Bekki wondered if that's the way
it is for everybody. There's this whole other part of us
watching, collecting, waiting to be written to, to be asked
questions of, to be listened to. Bekki ran her fingers across

the written words in the notebook, as if she wanted to feel them with all of her; to say 'hello' and shake hands.

She was so glad she'd had a spare notebook that day in the garden of the holiday cottage. Bekki didn't feel alone anymore because she wasn't. Nor was Rebecca, and now, nor was Alice. It felt good. Nothing was written in the notebooks for several days afterwards. Instead, the time was spent just being... except for the three hours she spent watching her favourite soap on TV, obviously. Well, you can't change everything at once.

During this time, Bekki sent a paperback copy of *The Little Prince* as a gift to Louis. He'd be twelve years old now and she realised that she couldn't remember exactly when his birthday was. He'd moved out of London to Brighton with his mum, Daisy, Bekki's old friend, when his parents got divorced. They'd all been so close once upon a time. Childless friends slip out of the lives of those who become parents far too easily and too often. Inside the book, Bekki slipped a black and white postcard bearing a photo of a dog wearing sunglasses on the front. Louis loved dogs. She remembered that much. On the back of the postcard Bekki wrote:

'For Louis from your useless godmother. I'm sorry I missed your birthday. I hope you like the book. And tell your mum I'm sorry for being such a hopeless friend.

Lots of Love, Auntie Bekki x'

Chapter 6

The next veil slipped off quietly when no-one was watching. It only became apparent when it was tested. It's easy for a person to say that they've changed until something comes along to actually test it. Then we find out if the change is real or just words. Like those people in that lottery syndicate who put a pound in every week for years until they won the jackpot and started suing each other because one forgot to put their pound in and another came into it after everybody else. Such a test came about in a seemingly mundane way, but it was a good challenge because it was real. Like the lottery people, it was about money. That's about as real as it gets.

The advertising agency that Bekki had worked for were either extremely generous or had an incompetent accounts department. Either way, they paid Bekki three month's salary and twelve day's holiday pay three weeks after she had resigned. At first Bekki was delighted with the windfall and thought she'd just say nothing. She could plead ignorance if someone should spot the mistake down the line. However, after two days she began to struggle with her new self and thought of what Alice might say - because she was bound to know. After all, she had quit her job because it was all lies. She didn't want to be responsible for yet more deceit being added to the pile. With that in mind, she decided to call the accounts department at the agency and come clean.

The slightly bored, edging towards disappointed, voice of Stacey from accounts answered the phone: 'Good morning, Pitch Perfect Promotions, can I help you?' This disappointed edge was the cumulative effect on Stacey as a consequence of the enormous alteration that she saw in people's faces when they asked her what she did for a living. First, they would look impressed and fascinated when she told them 'I work for an advertising agency in Soho.' This would quickly change to no longer impressed nor particularly bothered when she said '…in the accounts department.' After the seventh time, these reactions in others had caused the permanent quality of low self-esteem that weighed heavily in the timbre of Stacey's voice every time she answered the phone. This was now fixed into her whole demeanour, relating not only to her job but to her whole purpose for being alive on this planet. It was like coming fourth in an Olympic marathon by three-hundredths of a second every single working day of her life.

Bekki didn't notice any of this. She was busy trying to do the right thing by both Alice and her desire for a greater conscience. 'Hi, this is Bekki Reeves, I worked for Pitch Perfect until recently.'

'Oh, yes?' said Stacey, 'which department?'

'Copywriting department. I was an office admin.'

Stacey did the same as almost everybody else did to *her* when she told them how she earned her living. At first, she was impressed bordering on jealous, then she 'humphed' a little to herself as Bekki went down in her estimation. She was only dealing with a humble office admin. Not part of the real creative team at all. She was lower than an accountant. She might as well have worked in Tesco's. 'How can I help?' asked Stacey, recovering her self-esteem just a tiny bit.

'The thing is, I gave a month's notice when I resigned but I didn't work it, so I'm not sure if I should have got paid any extra. I think I should have only got paid till the end of the month,' explained Bekki. 'I was also due some holiday pay and I think I got all of that, so that's okay, but there seems to be at least double what I was expecting on my last pay slip and it's gone into my bank account already. Can you check it for me in case there's been a mistake, please?'

Stacey could now pull herself up to full sitting height in her ergonomic, Fairtrade swivel chair. 'I very much doubt that there's been a mistake. We're all fully trained, highly qualified accountants here. And anyway, the computer would have flagged it up. We've got Sage.'

'Oh, sure, I'm not saying it's anybody's fault…'

'Of course it isn't. We're fully digitised.'

'Could you just check for me anyway? Just to put my mind at rest?'

Stacey was relishing the sudden feeling of power. Hers would be the final say in this conversation, for once. 'Okay, I'll check it on the system for you. What did you say your name was?'

'Bekki Reeves.'

'Ummm… can't see that name. There was a Rebecca Reeves on the system.'

'Yes, that's me. Bekki's short for Rebecca.'

'It would be helpful if you gave me the right name in the first instance, otherwise how do I know it's really you?' Stacey was enjoying herself now. 'This is sensitive, personal information that you're asking for. We can't give it to just anybody over the phone. It's for your own security as well as ours, you know.'

As Stacey's stature became bloated and sat with more weight on the swivel chair, Bekki began to wish that she'd just kept the money and not bothered calling at all. But the promise of a new Rebecca/Bekki/Alice going into the future with a clean slate was too important to let go of for the sake of an accounts assistant with low self-esteem and a point to prove. Bekki took a deep breath, decided that the new life being born had to be an honest one, and answered all of Stacey's security questions, even if it meant ultimately losing some much-needed cash.

Bekki gave Stacey her full name and address. Then she stated her date of birth and national insurance number. Then she told her the exact starting and leaving dates with regard to her employment at Pitch Perfect Promotions. Then she told Stacey her hair colour, mother's maiden name and which desk she had sat at in the copywriter's office. Then she told Stacey her favourite film and the name of the person who had snogged Mike Lewis, the European Accounts Manager, behind the alcoholic slushie machine at the Christmas party. It was Eric from IT. She knew the last few questions were unnecessary and, quite frankly, bordered on telephone bullying, but she allowed Stacey her day in the sun.

'Right, well that all seems to be in order. You *do* appear to be the Rebecca Reeves who worked for us until recently.'

Us? It was *us* now, thought Bekki. Stacey was standing proudly on a pinnacle of her own self-satisfaction and the joy of it could be heard down the phone with all its bells and whistles.

'So, do you think there's been a mistake with my final pay or not?' asked Bekki.

'Not. I mean, no, that's not possible. It appears that you have been paid everything that you're due. We don't owe you anything more. Sorry.'

'I wasn't saying that you owed me anything, I was just...'

'Well, that's good, because I can assure you that we don't.'

'You're absolutely sure that there's no extra payment? Some kind of severance pay or golden handshake?'

'I don't think so.' Stacey stifled a snigger at the idea, but not very successfully. 'You left us, remember?' There was the 'us' bomb again.

'Right. So, I've had absolutely everything I'm due, and nobody owes anyone a penny?' Bekki just had to triple check. 'Nothing at all. We're all square as far as wages are concerned.'

'Yep, that's right. I can put it in an email for you, if you want.'

'No, that's okay.' Bekki's mind was whirring. Maybe she should get something in writing. Or maybe that would give Stacey a chance to triple check herself and come up with a different answer. How would that play out? Before Bekki could decide, the awkward silence was broken by the increasingly confident Stacey.

'Was there anything else you wanted, because we are rather busy here today.'

'No, no, that's all. Thank you very much for your help.'

'You're welcome. Thanks for calling.' Stacey put the phone down before Bekki could have the last word. And boy, did that feel good to her. That, plus the satisfaction of confirming that it had been Eric from I.T. behind the alcoholic slushie machine all along. 'I knew it,' she said out loud, although there was no one in her office to hear.

Bekki didn't mind that Stacey got the last word. It was turning out to be a good day. She had been honest. Alice would be proud. There had been an opportunity for deceit, a choice to be made, a test of integrity, and Bekki had passed. She knew that she must have been overpaid, she told the company so and checked it more than once. The company, or rather their representative, was too stubborn and too proud to admit that they could have possibly made a mistake, so Bekki could keep the money. That's what really happened with Stacey. Sometimes people will accept a loss as long as it looks like they've won.

Before writing up this small victory in Notebook Number One, Bekki just had to tell someone what had happened, so she phoned her little sister. Jane wasn't as impressed as Bekki hoped she might be.

'What?!' exclaimed Jane down the phone with no little derision. 'You got some free cash, completely innocently, without having to steal it from anyone, and you tried to give it *back*?'

'You're missing the point,' said Bekki. And then, on a different note, she added: 'Are you eating something?'

'Yeah,' said Jane, 'it's a Belvita. I'm trying to lose a stone before I go to Magaluf.'

'Is it working?'

'Well it would have if I hadn't just eaten seven of the delicious little buggers. It's the chocolate chip ones.'

Bekki was getting distracted. She tried to pull herself back to her victory. 'Anyway, the point is I could have just said nothing and kept the cash, but I didn't.'

Jane finished eating Belvita number eight and cleared her throat of the dry biscuit. 'That's what I would have done. In fact, that's what any normal person would have done.'

Bekki wouldn't be swayed. 'What? You would have just kept money that you knew you hadn't earned? Money that didn't rightly belong to you? What if they found out and chased you for it? How would that have looked?'

'I would have just pleaded ignorance and said I hadn't noticed it going into my account. Most people never check their statements these days.' Bekki could hear Jane rifling about in the packet, hunting for one more Belvita. The little 'tut' in the background suggested there were none to be had.

'Well, I didn't plead ignorance,' said Bekki, a little annoyed with herself for getting defensive. 'I did the right thing and owned up. That money shouldn't have been paid to me. It wasn't mine.'

'Is anyone at the company going to miss it?'

'That's not the point.'

'Whatever,' said Jane.

Bekki tried one more angle: 'I thought you'd be proud of your sister for being honest in the face of temptation. I'm trying to set a good example and you're not even a tiny bit impressed.'

'Look,' said Jane, 'I don't get what you're trying to teach

65

me. You've ended up with the money in your account anyway, right?'

'Right.' Bekki didn't like where this was going.

'Money that wasn't meant to be yours, and isn't going to be missed, yeah?'

'Yes, but...'

'So, what's your point?'

There was a short pause while Bekki tried to gather her point into an inspiring sentence that would cause the required reaction in her sister. This was the best she could come up with: 'I guess my point is that I had a choice. I could be upfront and honest or deceitful and greedy, and I chose *not* to be dishonest, even if I wasn't going to get caught, that's all. I thought you'd be proud of me.'

'Okay. Nice one, sis. Is that what you want to hear?'

Before Bekki could say 'Thank you,' Jane continued.

'The point is though, in the end, it didn't make any difference whether you were honest or not. You've still got a load of cash in your bank account that you shouldn't have had – it's alright for some. So, if you've just called me to gloat...'

'No,' said Bekki, 'that's not it at all. I called to tell you, as your big sister, that sometimes we have the opportunity to swim against the tide; to be honest, even in a small way, in a world where most other people would just lie and be proud of it, do you know what I mean? It can be done, it should be done, and it felt good, that's all.' By now it was not sounding like it felt good at all.

'Whatever,' conceded Jane. Then she dealt the killer blow: 'But if you really want to swim against the tide and be different to everybody else, you know what you've gotta do, don't ya?'

Bekki didn't want Jane to tell her, but she asked anyway. 'What have I got to do?'

'You should take that money out of your bank account right now and give it to charity. Or you could give it to me and I'll spend it for you in Magaluf. And while I'm there I can raise a glass or two to your honesty and decency!' Jane let out a big laugh then a short, dry cough. There was a little Belvita crumb tickling her throat.

Bekki wanted to swear into the phone as loudly as possible at this point, but she thought that would just make Jane laugh even harder and then possibly choke to death on a chocolate chip breakfast bar. Instead, she stuck out her tongue down the phone, as if her sister could see her. Of course, Jane probably wasn't looking down the phone at all but in the back of the cupboard for more Belvitas. What Bekki did finally say was, 'When did you get so smart, little sis?'

'I always was. Ain't you ever noticed? You might be the creative one, but I've got all the street smarts. Anyway, was there anything else you wanted to talk about, because I've got to get down to the Post Office and pick up some euros.'

'No, that was it,' said Bekki. 'Have a good time in Magaluf - but not too good.'

'Cheers,' said Jane. 'See you when I get back, Bekks. Love ya!'

'Love ya too,' and Bekki put the phone down.

Shit! Jane was right. What difference did it make? It might have been a small test, but it seemed like such a big victory at the time. It was true that most people would have said nothing and kept it, like when someone gives you too much change in a shop and you pretend not to notice. They can probably afford to lose it, can't they? Can they? Who is it really hurting?

Then Bekki had a breakthrough. It was a small start but it just might lead to something big. It would, however, take a long time. She got out her notebook and wrote a letter to Alice. If Bekki had written it before she phoned Jane it would have been very different. But here it was...

Dear Alice,

Well, I've started going forwards. Today is the beginning of the new and the end of the old. Today has been interesting, so far. I've learnt something big and this is it: it seems to me that most people lie most of the time. We lie about everything, big and small. And even though we all know that there are consequences to our deceptions, we do it anyway because we gamble on never being caught. It's a big gamble. The trouble is that lies that don't get found out affect the liar more than anyone else because... they KNOW they are a liar. How do we all live with that fact? I'll tell you. We lie to ourselves about it! Isn't that amazing? We tell ourselves it's okay because everyone else does it too. I'm going to start from today to try and be honest with myself. If I can't be honest with myself, I can't be honest with anybody else. I don't think it's going to be easy. I'll let you know how I get on.

Love,

Bekki x

On the same page of the notebook, in smaller writing and with a lighter hand, was a note from Alice:

Dear Bekki,
   Good luck with that.
   Alice

After her letter was written, Bekki went to the bank, drew out the extra money that she'd been paid in error and sent the whole lot to the Guide Dogs for the Blind Association. It wasn't easy to do, she very nearly talked herself out of it, but she did it all the same. It made her feel both righteous and foolish at the same time. There was also a little piece of her that knew this was just the first clumsy step on a very long path. She decided not to tell anyone else about what had happened, at least for now. They wouldn't understand. In fact, they'd probably laugh or ask her for a loan.

Later that same afternoon, Stacey from Pitch Perfect Promotions walked round the corner to the Hare & Bicycle to treat herself to a pub lunch. There she met a thirty-five-year-old insurance executive called Ian who asked her what she did for a living. 'I work for an advertising agency in Soho,' she said.

'Oh, really?' he said, 'that sounds fascinating. What's your role in the company?'

'I'm a trouble-shooter,' said Stacey. Ian was so impressed that he bought her a mung bean lasagne and a large glass of Merlot. They've been dating ever since.

Chapter 7

Day One of Bekki's anti-deception mission was a breeze. This was because she'd managed to catch a nasty cold and didn't go outside the front door or speak to another human being for the whole day.

Bekki's one-bedroom flat was on the third floor of an ex-council block, overlooking the Grand Union Canal in Islington. They don't build social housing like that anymore. In fact, they hardly build any social housing at all. By the year two-thousand, three quarters of the flats in Bekki's block were no longer classed as council housing. Gone forever. Sold with massive discounts to ex-tenants who had cashed in and sold up as soon as they could, to move to Essex and the cheaper parts of Kent. Bekki bought her flat from one of its previous council tenants on the insistence of her parents. Despite being a bargain for Bekki, the ex-owner made a killing and moved to Canvey Island. 'You'll never get a better deal,' her mother had said at the time, and she was right. Who knew that selling off affordable, secure council properties would cause a severe housing crisis in Britain twenty years down the line? Actually, lots of people knew, but there was little they could do about it.

It was easier to define what is called 'the working classes' when Rebecca was a little girl. Even easier to define it when her grandmother was young. It referred to the majority of the population who worked in the skilled and unskilled trades doing the kind of work that gets your hands dirty. Or those who worked in the lower paid jobs that required no qualifications, like shop assistants, cleaners and coal miners, and the slightly better paid jobs that also required no qualifications, like policemen and criminals.

Whether they lived in the city or the countryside, back then the working classes usually couldn't afford to own their own homes, and mostly they believed it was a dream that could never be realised. That was one of the class boxes to tick. They lived in council houses or cheap rental properties or had jobs that provided accommodation, like nurses and farm hands and soldiers. This all changed in the nineteen-eighties when Margaret Thatcher shifted the goalposts and decided that people who lived in council houses should be allowed to buy them. Presumably she thought that this would help to keep them exactly where they were so that they wouldn't be tempted to spread out to the better suburbs and rural idylls. Once they owned their own roof and four walls, their aspirations would be satisfied and they'd all behave themselves. It didn't quite turn out that way. Instead, this new rule unleashed a property-ladder frenzy as ambitions to own more than just a little piece of land with a house or flat on it were born in the lowest of social climbers. The discounted prices to council tenants were so low that it would be a shame not to cash in and make a profit, like a true child of Thatcher. This meant that most of the housing stock reserved for the poorest was lost forever. It also created a new breed of working class Tory voters in Essex and the cheaper parts of Kent who had never voted Conservative before. They and their new party were happy for years.

Many governments since Margaret Thatcher have promised to replace affordable housing for the millions that genuinely need it. None of them have done it. The consequence of this is that it's very difficult to figure out where the working classes now live, rendering it almost impossible to keep them in their place, away from the better suburbs and rural idylls. Nowadays you're likely to find them almost anywhere, living mortgage-free in Colchester or Cardiff off the proceeds of their council house sales, or with large mortgages in Surrey with three adult children still at home because they have no council flats of their own in which they can afford to live without sponging off their parents.

When Bekki's parents were young and still working class, it was extremely rare to know more than one person from your street who went to university. It was only necessary to be educated until the age of sixteen in order to be a useful, economic contributor to society. Or fifteen if you wanted to be a footballer, musician, or plasterer. Today the universities are full of people who are the first in their family to have the time or money to be able to study for a degree. There is now more equality in higher education than ever in Britain's history. Anybody, no matter what their background or social status might be, is now perfectly entitled to a massive student debt that will never be fully repaid in their lifetime.

When Bekki's notebooks first began, the term 'working class' had become so blurred that nobody really knew what it meant. Ironically, it was middle and upper-class artists and poets that bought up the old council houses in some of the worst parts of London, thus making them so trendy and desirable that only politicians and foreign oligarchs could now afford them. The over-privileged moved into the damp workrooms of old sweatshops in Hoxton, and the taxi drivers and cleaners moved to leafy avenues in Barnet. That's where Bekki's parents now lived. Thirty minutes' drive from their old council house in Highbury, but a million miles away in terms of living standards. Out were the dodgy covered walkways and communal bins, and in was the gazebo and the stork-garnished water feature. Her dad still drove his black cab into London four times a week, but there was no need for the lucrative but unpleasant night shifts anymore. He could pick and choose when he worked.

Saddled with a mortgage at the age of twenty-one, Bekki had often wondered if it was the right thing to do. On an almost monthly basis, her mother would email her links to property websites with brief messages attached, like: 'Prices up by four percent in your postcode this quarter, Rebecca,' and other such notes of upwardly mobile encouragement. Now that Bekki was jobless, she thought it might be time to actually click through to one of those websites, but not today. She didn't feel up to proving her mother right. That was always exhausting. And she had a cold.

Bekki enjoyed decorating the flat when she first moved in. It was a shabby chic blend of pastel blues and greens with an eclectic collection of pre-loved furniture dotted around. Half of the furniture had come from her beloved grandmother's house. The old lady had passed away on the same day that Bekki got the keys to the flat. This was an unfortunate coincidence but a huge help in getting started. The art deco sideboard and sofa that her mother had always hated when she was growing up was now the height of on-trend interior design and Bekki found it comforting. She snuggled down on the sofa and wrapped her grandma's crocheted throw around her shoulders. It smelled of barley sugar and lavender. She liked it. She remembered the steaming mugs of honey and lemon garnished with cinnamon sticks that her grandmother would make for her as a child whenever she was poorly and how they always seemed to dry up a runny nose. Her mind wandered to thoughts of cold remedy delivery services where you could phone up and get a visit from a grandma bearing hot toddies, soup, and soft tissues. There must be a market for that. It was surprising that nobody had yet thought of it. There's money to be made there.

When her favourite soap came on at seven-thirty, Bekki asked herself, 'Do I really want to waste half an hour of my life watching a TV show that bases all of its story lines on secrets and lies?' Her answer was: 'Yes. I feel poorly and it's my TV version of comfort food.' Bekki thought about this for at least two minutes and decided it was a perfectly honest answer. No deceit there whatsoever. She watched the soap while eating tomato soup and toasted cheese sandwiches that she had to make for herself because there was no grandma delivery service yet. There really was money to be made there. Later, she checked the kitchen cupboards and was delighted to find a jar full of cinnamon sticks and a squirty, lemon-shaped plastic container of some kind of citric acid. It was still within its sell by date, and the cinnamon sticks were only a couple of months over. There was always honey in the cupboard. Bekki liked it on toast. She put the kettle on, made a steaming mug of grandma's cold cure, and fell asleep under the crochet throw. Day One was a success. Only the rest of her life to go, however many days that might turn out to be.

Day Two was when the big challenge came. The scale of this cannot be over-estimated. It was the biggest test that Bekki was likely to ever face in her quest to stop lying forever. Her mother phoned.

Bekki didn't have Caller I.D. on her landline, which meant that it wasn't possible to prepare herself for the call. Her mother refused to call on her mobile phone as Joyce from the W.I. had told her that it cost five pounds a minute, and Joyce's son was in I.T.

'Hello, Rebecca darling, it's me.'

'Hi, mum. I was just about to call you.'

That was the first lie. It came out of Bekki's mouth before she had time to think. Old habits die hard, and deceit is one of the oldest habits in the world. She was really pissed off with herself for caving so quickly. Of course, she couldn't let her mother know how angry she was with herself. That would only lead to difficult questions. Bekki would have to pretend that everything was fine, as she always did when she spoke to her mother.

'How are you, dear?'

'I'm fine, mum.' And there it was. That was lie number two. It crept in so effortlessly that Bekki didn't even notice. Alice did, of course. She noticed everything.

'You don't sound fine to me. Are you sick, Rebecca?'

'It's just a cold. It probably sounds worse than it is.' That was true. It really was just a snotty cold.

'Lots of liquids and an early night for you, I think.'

'Yes, mum. I will.'

'Is that why you're not at work today?'

'Ah, well...' Bekki paused to clear her throat, blow her nose, and play for time. 'I was going to tell you about that.'

This was not strictly a lie. She *was* going to tell her mother that she'd quit a well-paid job in a cool part of London because she'd had an epiphany about the hypocritical, self-destructive path that the human race was hurtling down. She just hadn't planned to do it *yet*. Or while she had a cold. Or until she had found another job.

'And *what*, exactly, were you going to tell me?' her mother pressed.

'Well...' Bekki blew her nose loudly once more in the hope of receiving some sympathy. 'I know you'll understand once I explain.'

'No need,' interrupted her mother. 'I've just spoken to Jane and she told me all about it. What were you thinking, Rebecca?'

Bekki pulled herself up in the armchair she'd been lounging on in her *Wonder Woman* pyjamas. 'Whatever Jane told you is probably only half the story, if that.' She made a mental note never to confide in her sister again. Of course, she wouldn't keep this promise, but that wasn't really a lie. More like an over-ambitious intention. Like every time she'd bought a new garment that was a size too small that she would shed a few pounds to fit into. There were currently three such items at the back of the wardrobe.

Her mother continued before Bekki had a chance to either tell the truth or rack up her score by one more lie. She told Bekki exactly why she was wrong to quit her job, how she was much luckier than so many other people (who she didn't specify), plus herself at Bekki's age (which she specified a lot), then she seamlessly shoe-horned in the fact that her daughter was still unmarried and childless at the age of twenty-eight (despite this having nothing to do with her employment status), and finished by asking the rhetorical question that all siblings dread: 'Why can't you be more like your brother?'

Bekki's little brother, Jimmy, was then twenty-one-years old and had just completed a degree in Media Studies at Manchester University. His ambition, or so he told his parents, was to go into TV production, probably at the BBC, and preferably, his mother hoped, with some connection to Richard Madeley, even though he was on ITV. She admired the willowy, flicky-haired TV personality in a way that made her children a little uncomfortable.

What Bekki wanted to say to her mother was: *Jimmy's not the golden child you think he is. A): he didn't get a first-class degree, he got a third, and that was only because he cheated. He lied and photo-shopped the certificate you've got hanging on the dining room wall above the Hostess Trolley. B) He has no intention of working for the BBC or ITV, even if he could. His only ambition is to run a bar in Brighton so that he can drink for free. C): He spent most of the allowance dad gave him on weed at Uni and owes Tim Two-Tasers five hundred quid and a crate of tequila. And D): he came out as gay to everyone except you last February at the Manchester Pride while dressed as Bette Midler, and dad's too scared to tell you that he knows. I've got photos to prove it.'*

Of course, Bekki said none of this to her mother. Using all of her will-power, she held back this tsunami of information, assisted by the wad of tissues up her nose. But she didn't lie. What she did say in response to her mother's question was succinct and true. 'I'm not Jimmy.'

'That's right, you're not,' her mother agreed. 'He's found his direction in life. When are you going to find yours?'

There was a brief silence on Bekki's end of the phone. Then there was another loud nose-blowing episode, concluded with a short, sad sniff. Her mother softened her tone. 'I'm worried about you, Rebecca. I only say these things because I care, darling. You know that, don't you?'

Yeah, sure you do, said Bekki inside her head. 'I know, mum,' she lied out loud.

Most people forgive their parents when they reach the age of forty or fifty. Some things can never be forgiven because they are simply too traumatic or unnatural. Fortunately, the latter is only the experience of a luckless minority. For everybody else, it takes the birth of their own children and their development into teenagers, with all the pride and disappointment that brings, for a person to finally accept their parents weren't perfect. They could only do their best with what they had, and that acceptance breeds forgiveness. For those without children, it becomes easy to see all the things their friends have missed out on simply because they chose to expand the population with somebody that looks like them but will never actually be them. What they miss out on are things like sleep, money, spontaneity, freedom, bouncy pelvic floors, and more sleep. The sympathy, or perhaps superiority, that this engenders in those who are smug, helps the middle-aged child understand that it must have been really difficult to be their particular mother and/or father. This then breeds forgiveness in most people eventually.

Mrs Pamela Reeves was a pretty average mother: interfering, overbearing, caring, sacrificing, judgemental, nurturing, and fiercely protective. Very average, in fact. For twenty-eight-year-old Bekki, it was only the negative qualities that she saw. She hadn't yet come to appreciate the others.

Mr Reeves was equally average as a father: repressed, childish, loyal, hardworking, affectionate, lazy, uninterested, and fiercely protective. He never, ever phoned Bekki unless it was a massive emergency. Even a medium-sized emergency couldn't get him to pick up the phone. He would, however, call out silly nonsense and affectionate greetings from the other side of the room whenever her mother called and he was at home. He never, ever signed birthday cards either. His wife always did that. She never asked permission, just wrote his name in block capitals under her own and underscored both with a single 'x'. They were old school.

This particular phone call ended with Bekki vowing to go and see her parents very soon, perhaps for Sunday lunch, and then promising not to do anything rash without speaking to her mother first. Only part of this was a lie, and then only a half-lie at that. Of course, she would go and visit mum and dad. 'Soon' would just be a bit fluid, that's all. As for the second promise, Bekki couldn't see anything rash in her current decision-making at all. If anything, she though the changes she had already made were well overdue. She knew that she had lied, though. That bit was hard. In fact, this whole lying thing was much bigger than she had envisaged.

Within a couple of days, the snotty cold was almost gone. It was helped on its way by the copious consumption of hot lemon, honey, and out-of-date cinnamon sticks, topped up with large glugs of dark rum. Her spin on grandma's recipe. It worked a treat. The hours spent lounging around in pyjamas with these delicious mugs of medicine had allowed time to think without interruption. Tackling deception - a major virus infecting the human race - was probably too big a challenge for a newbie, for someone at the very beginning of their path to enlightenment. There must be an easier place to start.

As the need for clean tissues subsided, and before the skin had grown back on the sides of her nostrils, Bekki penned a letter in her notebook:

Dear Alice,

The world, and all the people in it, are stuffed full of lies and deceit, and I'm no different. It's shocking! There's so much of it that it's hard to even tell when it's happening until it's too late. We're all wading in it up to our waists so that even our wellies can't stop it… sorry, that analogy doesn't really work, but you know what I mean.

I told you in my last letter that I intend to tackle this flood of deception (still trying to make the analogy work!) and stop LYING, both to myself

81

and to everybody else. But I realise that I'm not yet
ready for such a big challenge. I want to change,
and I already am, but I also need to be realistic. I
want to start with something a little more simple
and straightforward so that I can have a success
and build on it. Trying to stop lying by going cold
turkey can only lead to failure. So, I've decided to
stop smoking instead.
   Yours with honesty,
   Bekki xx

Alice did reply, almost straight away, but the response
was even briefer than the last one.

Dear Bekki,
   Again: Good luck!
   Alice

Bekki gave up smoking for three days. In that time,
she had an argument with the postman about junk mail,
ate four family packs of Maltesers, and saved fifteen
pounds minus the cost of the Maltesers. This was, of
course, all happening twenty-four years ago at the start of
the twenty-first century. Bekki doesn't smoke anymore. It
took her nine months to finally quit. Giving up deception
would take much longer.

Chapter 8

So far, we have only covered the first half of Notebook Number One and everything that happened during the time that it was being written in. The second half is amusing to look back on now. It's mostly made up of what can be most accurately described as resolutions. And just like the ones that so many people make at the start of each new year, Bekki pretty much broke all of her new life resolutions within days, some within hours, of making them.

To remove the need to duplicate half a notebook, and all the paper that might waste, here are some selected highlights from all of the decisions decided and promises made, along with the outcome of each. The times in brackets denote how long the resolution was kept before Bekki broke it.

'I will exercise for at least half an hour every day.' *(fifteen minutes)*

Halfway through the first exercise session, Bekki stubbed her toe on the coffee table, went to the freezer to fetch a bag of peas for the swelling, found half a tub of rum and raisin ice-cream, ate it all, and didn't exercise again until halfway through Notebook Number Two.

'I will meditate every morning for ten minutes.' (two weeks)

At this point, Bekki had absolutely no experience of meditation, but she thought it was the kind of thing a person on a path of enlightenment should know how to do. The only person she knew who had any experience in the field - quite literally - was her sister, who had done a taster session at Glastonbury under the influence of some dodgy-tasting fungi. Unfettered by this, Jane advised Bekki that the best way to meditate was to pick a fruit or vegetable of her choice and simply focus on that with her eyes closed, blocking everything else out of her mind. Sitting cross-legged on the floor would also help this, although Jane didn't explain why. She couldn't explain why because she had made that bit up. When she had her one and only meditation experience, she'd spent most of it lying on the ground behind a falafel tent, contemplating asparagus while wearing a smiley-face t-shirt, a bandana, and not much else.

Bekki chose to visualise a strawberry because that was her favourite fruit. This was not a good choice. Every time she tried to meditate, and within seconds of closing her eyes, her mind would be filled with images of thick, strawberry milkshakes, creamy pink ice-cream, and bowls full of the delicious little rascals dripping with cream. Before even half of the allotted ten minutes had passed, Bekki would be up from her lotus position on the living room rug, and off to the fridge to satisfy her rumbling stomach. If there was nothing red and fruity to be had there, she would be off down the shops before you could say 'Hatha Yoga.'

Bekki did eventually get to grips with the art of meditation, but not for another couple of years, and not until she had found some proper instruction. By the end of Notebook Number One, however, Bekki had an Angel Delight addiction and was carrying an extra five pounds, mostly around her hips, which incidentally was where Jane had been wearing her bandana at Glastonbury.

I will not judge or criticise other people lest I be judged. (forty-five seconds)

Yes, Bekki did use the word 'lest' in a moment of literary exuberance and completely out of character. And no, she didn't think this one through at all. What she should have done was approach this particular issue with caution and a lot of realism. The quality of criticism - which really isn't a quality at all - is as ingrained and destructive in the human race as deception is. Tackling such a big thing so early on was asking for failure. Bekki should also have made sure the TV was switched off when she was writing this particular resolution in her notebook, but it wasn't. The volume wasn't even turned down.

The show that happened to be on at this sensitive time in Bekki's development was what is called, quite inaccurately, a 'reality TV show.' This particular one featured a herd of scantily clad, impossibly tanned, young people in a millionaire's mansion on the Costa del Sol. It was a kind of human zoo where the inmates were waxed within an inch of their lives before being locked up in a pool-side villa with a bunch of summer clothes that were all two sizes too small. Bekki finished writing her promise to remove judgement and criticism from her life, took a sip of tea, glanced up at the TV and said, out loud: 'OMG! Look at the size of her arse! Look out, everyone - that thong is gonna blow!!' She laughed out loud to herself, took another sip of tea, and settled down to watch the rest of the episode. As the end titles scrolled across the screen, Bekki was devastated to realise what she'd spent the last half an hour doing. This particular resolution is still visible in Notebook Number One, but an angry black line was drawn through it at that point. Above this line was simply written the word: 'Bollocks!'

This is just a small selection of the intentions and resolutions that Bekki tried to master. There were others, just as bold, such as 'The expansion of memory', 'The reduction of sleep', and the highly ambitious 'Removal of greed.' They all suffered similar fates.

Bekki didn't write anything further in that notebook for another month. In that time, she saw her savings go down and her food bills go up. Some people starve themselves when they're depressed, and some people feed. Both are forms of self-punishment for feeling bad and not knowing how to fix it. Very few people continue eating their meals as normal at these times. Depression enjoys this. Bekki was a feeder and her depression was becoming as heavy as she was.

By the time Notebook Number One was written in again, Bekki was feeling very low. She hadn't been out of the flat or seen another human being for a week, if you don't count the pizza delivery man. Enough was enough. She picked up her pen and wrote:

Dear Alice,

I'm very sad and I don't know what to do. It's so hard to change and I really, really want to - honest. But no matter what I try, I fail miserably. How did I get to be like this? I'm full of judgement and deception and self-loathing. How does this happen? How do we stop it? Is this it? Am I just going to go round and round in circles of over-intention and failure?

I'm STUCK! Please help me.
Bekki

For the first time in months, Alice replied with more than just a sentence. It didn't happen straight away. It came after another twenty-four hours of Bekki wallowing in ice-cream, reality TV, and misery.

Dear Bekki,

You might be feeling despondent right now, but what you can't see is that you're in the perfect place to begin the journey that you're looking for. It's not just a journey, it's the biggest adventure you'll ever go on, because you are heading towards the self that you have decided to be and not the accidental self that's been created by everything and everyone around you.

Before you can change direction, you need to come to a stop and adjust the compass. That's where you are. Here are a couple of tips to help you on your way:

Firstly, don't expect to get where you want to be in an instant. Time travel hasn't been invented yet.

Start small and build on the little successes. Instead of eliminating all deception or criticism from your life, aim to reduce it by one percent. Then, when you've achieved that, reduce it by another one percent, then another. Imagine a world where hate and bigotry was reduced by ten percent every year. How amazing would that be in ten years' time?

Secondly, you are not alone. It might feel like you're the only person in the world who is sick of all the lies and ignorance that exists, but this is not true. Almost everybody feels the same way, they just don't know how to change it either. Conformity is a dangerous thing. It's also a very comfortable and familiar thing. What you're feeling is the iron ring that it weighs people down with. Talk to friends. Ask people how they feel. You might be surprised. Perhaps together you can start something better to conform to.

Thirdly, here is a very big secret: There are two things that depression cannot stand. One is understanding. Try to look at it from the outside and recognise that it is not you, as depression would like you to believe. It's just something passing through you that causes you to behave like something other than yourself. Don't be fooled. The other thing it can't stand is humour. Depression hates to be laughed at. It wants you to take it very, very seriously. This secret is simple to understand, but it takes a lot of time and practice to master. Keep going. You are at the start of something incredible.

With care and watchfulness,
Alice x

Bekki sat on the sofa, curled up in her grandma's crocheted throw. She read Alice's letter three times, and then decided it was worth a go. She had run out of ideas of her own. So, she switched on the TV, flicked through the channels and found, to her delight, an old Marx Brothers' movie. She loved those films. Her father was a big fan of the early comedy greats and would often spend Saturday mornings introducing his children to the likes of Laurel and Hardy, Charlie Chaplin, and Buster Keaton from his large video collection. The film on offer today was *Duck Soup*. That was her father's favourite, especially the famous silent mirror sequence. She knew it off by heart, but it never failed to make her smile.

Bekki reached for the phone and dialled the takeaway pizza place up the road. This time she ordered a nine-inch Margarita instead of a twelve-inch Hawaiian. It was a start. Like Alice said, start small and build on the little successes. Were nine inches ten percent smaller than twelve? If Bekki's maths was right, it was even greater than that.

The resolutions calmed down after this. They became far more practical, too, or at least some of them did. The last entry that Bekki wrote in Notebook Number One reads as follows:

The next stage of the journey:

Priority: Think carefully about where to live and what to do for income. London is very expensive when you're unemployed and surrounded by fast-food joints that deliver.

First Task: Get the flat valued.

Second Task: Look for a new home and new job

that allows the best ecology to enable me to continue the new life that I've started... before I run out of money! Must be somewhere more natural and less toxic for the soul; somewhere far from all the hypocrisy and greed of the rat race.

Places to research (house prices, visas, climate, etc.):

Thailand Bali

Ecuador New Zealand

Crete Suffolk

Third Task: Consider getting a cat. And a garden.

And that was the end of Notebook Number One.

Chapter 9

From the outside cover, Notebook Number Two looks very different to Notebook Number One. When Alice first started writing in the garden of that Suffolk holiday cottage, it was totally unplanned; a spontaneous revelation. She had found a loose-leaf pad in the owner's kitchen drawer and scribbled down her first urgent messages. She couldn't have known then that this would turn into a twenty-four-year relationship with the notebooks.

It was a few weeks before Bekki took herself to the big Paperchase store in Tottenham Court Road to choose a hardback, unlined black notebook to paste those first months' worth of random writings into. By the end of that notebook she was writing straight into its pages, wishing that she'd bought the ruled version with margins. Trying to write in straight lines on blank paper is both distracting and time-consuming. She didn't make that mistake again.

The exterior of Notebook Number One was covered in little creases and dents where it had been thrust in and out of handbags and onto bookshelves and thrown across rooms on at least three occasions. There was also an annoying tacky patch on the cover where Bekki had once placed a humorous - and the word is *not* used literally here - sticker, thought better of it, then attempted to peel it off without total success. The sticker had once said, 'I'm having my period and can therefore legally kill you.' Now there was just a rough smidge of grey-white paper that said 'od gal' with no explanation or apology.

By comparison, Notebook Number Two was pristine. A friendly-looking yellow cover with a white daisy pattern, ring bound to sit flat while writing, and pleasingly ruled with margins. The only annoying thing about this one was that it was ever so slightly taller than all the other notebooks. Mostly Bekki had written straight into this one, with just the occasional pasted-in entry when she was away from the book but just had to write something down on whatever scrap of paper might be to hand.

From Notebook Number Three onwards, a clear pattern had developed. Each one was the same brand, selected for the smoothness of the paper, their eco credentials, and variety of colours. Each was a different shade so that Bekki could pick out which number the book might be in the sequence with ease, should she wish to go back and re-read something that she had written. This hardly ever happened.

Notebook Number Two begins with a story rather than one of Bekki's usual letters or lists. It was written out beautifully in her best handwriting and with her favourite blue pen. Not all of the entries are written with such patience and attention to detail, but it's like that with most things. People tend to put things into new, empty places with care at first, like the first brushstroke on a canvas or the first shirt in a wardrobe. It's a satisfying feeling. Before long, though, things are getting shoved in wherever there's space and sometimes where there isn't.

Unlike a lot of Bekki's previous writings, she had done much preparation before jotting down this particular story. She had made copious notes in an exercise book that was normally kept for shopping lists and reminders, just so that she could get everything right in her head. Those notes are long gone and the finished story in Notebook Number Two is very detailed and a tad overwritten, spanning ten pages or more. Rather than reproduce it all here, I will relay a shorter version in my own words, which should have the same impact. Bekki was still learning how to write the way she wanted to. Remember, this was more than twenty years ago. She's much better at it nowadays.

It happened a short while after Notebook Number One was full. Bekki had completed her first task and had her Islington flat valued by a local estate agent. She was shocked at the asking price that they recommended. Her mother had been wrong. The property values in Bekki's neighbourhood had gone up even more than her mother had claimed in her most recent email. They had gone through the roof, no pun intended. It was time to sell up.

On her way back from the estate agent's office, Bekki decided to pop into her local supermarket for some essentials and a celebratory strawberry cheesecake. As she wheeled her shopping trolley out into the car park, she was dismayed at what she saw. She'd never noticed it so starkly. There were several covered trolley parks placed in convenient spots around the car park, mostly empty apart from bits of discarded packaging and cigarette butts. Everywhere else there were numerous abandoned shopping trolleys in random places where people had unloaded them and then left them to become someone else's problem.

'Thoughtless, selfish bastards,' thought Bekki. 'They just don't care about anyone but themselves.' But as she trundled her own trolley to the boot of her blue two-door Mini, she remembered her pledge to cut criticism and judgement by a further one percent this month. So, she hoisted her Bags For Life into the boot of the car and wheeled her trolley back into the nearest designated area. It slotted into another one with a satisfying 'click.'

Just then, a gruff male voice called out in her direction: 'Oi, sweetheart! What are you bothering to put your trolley away for? No other bugger does.'

Bekki spun around to see a large man in his fifties wearing a green t-shirt, slightly too small for him, and emblazoned with the unlikely slogan: 'I♥Disney.' He was loading large bags of shopping into his own car, four at a time. Bekki shrugged, thought for a moment, and then smiled broadly at the man. 'I'm doing it because I can,' she called back. 'We all have a choice, don't we?' And this, of course, was perfectly true.

The improbable Disney prince shrugged back and carried on loading his car. As Bekki drove out of the car park, she happened to glance in her rear-view mirror. She was delighted and rather surprised to see the man wheeling his trolley along the tarmac to click it in behind Bekki's in the designated area. She waved behind her, hoping to catch his eye, but the man didn't see her. That really didn't matter.

After Bekki had written down the story in Notebook Number Two, she left a few lines blank and then jotted down a letter to Alice. The handwriting was just as neatly written as it was in the original story. She was near the beginning of this notebook and still taking care, as mentioned before.

Dear Alice,

I wrote this story to show you that I have learned something. Not because I remembered to reduce criticism and judgement - which isn't easy, by the way, especially living round here - but because I have understood something that you said about 'conformity.'

It must have started with one person dumping their shopping trolley without bothering to put it away. Then someone saw this and thought, 'Why should I bother if they haven't? I'll do the same as them.' Then someone else, then someone else. Like you said, conformity is comfortable and very easy. All you have to do is follow the leader. No thinking required.

When the man saw me putting my shopping trolley away, he must have understood that there was another choice. I know that sounds obvious, but I reminded him that there was, didn't I? And then, the minute he put his trolley away there were two of us, not just me. Double the number of people taking a little extra care. Who knows? Maybe someone saw him do it, and then there were three, and four, and five…

The point is, he found something a little bit nicer to conform to for a moment. He made a choice. He thought about it and decided for himself whether to be considerate or not. Isn't that great? Mind you, he may have a preponderance to non-conformity, judging by his choice of t-shirt, but then I don't want to judge him. At least not by more than one percent less than I would have done yesterday. Is that right?

There was a pause in Bekki's letter then. She left a couple of blank lines to illustrate this. When she took up her pen again, the handwriting was smaller, as if she was writing with less confidence, which indeed was the case.

I've just had a thought: conformity is a chain. Each person is a link on the chain, but at any time you can break off and start a new chain, which is what I did with the shopping trolley. BUT all I did was start a new conformity, and I was chuffed with myself that I had, but it's still a kind of conformity. Is that bad?

You said that conformity is a dangerous thing and that it weighs you down. So, why did it feel so good to have been responsible for changing someone's behaviour? I bet ten thousand pounds that 'Disney man' would have just left his trolley in the middle of the car park if he hadn't seen me. At least what I did left the car park a bit tidier than it would have been without me. That's good, isn't it?

I'm confused. I started this letter saying that I understood conformity. Now I'm not so sure. Damn, this is hard!

Bekki x

Alice replied almost immediately.

Dear Bekki,

Sounds like you have indeed learned a lesson about conformity. Here's the missing bit that you're looking for: swapping one conformity for another is like swapping whisky for gin. It might taste different, but the outcome is the same - you become intoxicated. Did it matter that the man copied you rather than someone else? Did it feel good to be an instigator rather than a follower?

Of course, it's better to conform to something pleasant, but it's even better to choose to be neither a follower or a leader but to think for yourself. That's where freedom lies. I think that's what you're really after. I'm not sure if you realise that yet. Being self-decisive is the key, even if the decision is to do what everyone else is doing, because that's when responsibility for your own life begins. To conform is to abdicate responsibility.

Don't be too concerned about what others are doing or not doing. You cannot know their reasons without asking them first. Keep working on the judgement thing. It will help.

I'm sorry if this isn't the answer you were expecting. I'm sure you were hoping that I'd simply say 'Well done, Bekki.'

I will say that, if it's what you need. Ask yourself if you really do need it, and why.

Well done, Bekki. Keep going.
Alice.

Bekki looked at this letter for a long time. It made her frown as she read it. She wondered why there was no 'x' at the end. She wondered where the hell these letters were coming from. If they were coming from somewhere deep inside herself, why weren't they more flattering? Why weren't there more kisses at the end? Why wasn't she agreeing with herself all the time? She wanted Alice to say she was doing it right.

Everything needed more thought. Bekki didn't write in Notebook Number Two for a couple more months after that. She was busy. There was a flat to sell for an extortionate profit. It was now the beginning of November and definitely time to get out of London. She spent that difficult period over Christmas and New Year tidying up the flat, touching up bits of paintwork on scuffed walls and cupboards, and generally de-cluttering her life. This last process felt the most appropriate. All of this was a much welcome distraction from festive bank holidays without boyfriends and Christmas without office parties. Sure, there was a little space given to raising a glass here and there, but the next two months mostly passed by mercifully quickly.

The Christmas Number One that year was by Bob the Builder. On Boxing Day, whilst in a particularly playful mood, Bekki wrote a short letter to Alice:

Dear Alice,
'Can We Fix It?!'

Alice didn't reply to this letter. She had too much class. It sits there all alone in Notebook Number Two.

Future generations will have no idea what it means, or that it was meant to be a joke. Bekki never did like that stupid song.

Chapter 10

Stillard & Capstone Estate Agents, Islington Green branch, were very good at their job. They said so themselves to every client that walked through the door. 'If we can't sell your flat,' said Simon Stillard (real name) to Bekki when she walked through the door, 'then it isn't habitable. Dammit! Even if it *is* uninhabitable, we can *still* sell it! And that's a promise.'

This over-confidence was not misplaced and easily settled any doubts Bekki might have had. The flat went on the market in the middle of a cold snap in January. Within three days of it being advertised in the estate agent's window, it was sold for five thousand pounds over the asking price, despite it being so soon after the new year. The post-Christmas divorce rate probably helped. It usually does. Simon Stillard and Clint Capstone (also real name, astonishingly) took their commission and each bought a top-of-the-range electric go-kart with their respective half of the proceeds. Bekki now had just six to ten weeks to find somewhere else to live.

There were several calls from Bekki's mother around this time, all generously sprinkled with unwanted advice and examples of the bleeding obvious. During each call, Bekki practised reducing criticism and deception by another one percent, as she'd promised Alice. It wasn't easy. The conversations were all variations on the same theme and went something like this:

'You should have got valuations from at least three different estate agents, Rebecca. Honestly. How many times have I told you that?'

'It's done now, mum. I'm very happy with the price they got me. It's more than I was expecting.'

'I'm sure you could have got even more.'

'I'm really happy with the price.'

'I don't trust estate agents.'

'Nobody does, mum.'

'You still haven't told me where you're moving to.'

'I don't know yet. I'm working on it.'

'You haven't got much time, you know.'

'Yes, I know.'

'Probably no more than a couple of months.'

'I know.'

'You can always come home for a while. Your father wouldn't mind. I can move the pole out of the spare bedroom.'

It's worth clarifying here that the 'pole' that Mrs Reeves was referring to was a seven-foot high cylinder made of brushed steel and not an exchange student from Warsaw. Mr Reeves had installed it with much anticipation a couple of years previously, until he realised it was for his wife's latest exercise craze and not an attempt by her to spice up their marriage. Joyce from the W.I. had said that pole dancing was the best way to reduce floppy glutes. Pamela Reeves used it once, bruised her hip tackling a horizontal pivot, and never set a hand or a foot on it again. It now stood silently in the middle of the spare bedroom, naked and shiny like a sex show stage prop. The conversation continued…

'I didn't know you still had the pole, mum?'

'Only till your dad puts down the larch laminate.'

'I'll let you know if I get desperate.'

'I do worry about you, Rebecca. If only you were a bit more like your brother. I never have to worry about him.'

'I'll be fine, mum.'

'So, where are you thinking of going? You haven't got long, you know. Probably no more than a couple of months.'

Shit! Bugger! Bollocks! thought Bekki. 'Yes, I know, mum,' said Bekki.

A brief note would be useful here: Neither Rebecca nor Bekki used swear words very often in everyday language. They tended to be saved for situations where nothing else would do and so these words were far more potent whenever they were spoken out loud or written down. Rebecca and Bekki didn't object to swearing and never judged others for doing it, particularly when they did it properly. Bekki knew all the words and how to use them. She just lacked any kind of sophisticated pronunciation.

When Rebecca was eight years old, she found herself the butt of a cruel joke aimed at her by Lee Mossman after a particularly dramatic game of Off Ground Touch in the playground. She was so upset and angry that she screamed the 'F' word as a verb, followed by the word 'cheat,' right in his ratty little face. As the comment came out of her mouth, she realised with horror that it didn't sound cool or clever. Instead it sounded like her gran, who always over-pronounced the 'ng' at the end. Lee Mossman laughed so hard that a spit bubble came out of his nose. She punched him right on it as hard as she could and got a snotty fist and a letter sent home to her parents as a consequence. They were not pleased and she was grounded for a fortnight without TV privileges. She didn't mind being kept indoors for two weeks. Lee Mossman would forget about her in that time and move on to Sean Pilpeck with the lazy eye and the patch on his glasses. But she did miss the TV, especially *Top of the Pops*.

Despite spending those two weeks practising in front of the mirror in her bedroom while she was grounded, Rebecca could never make the really naughty words sound cool. So emotionally scarred was she by the experience that, from then onwards, she always tried to avoid swearing out loud in front of other people unless it was absolutely essential. It sounded much better in her head.

As much as Bekki hated to admit it, her mother was right about one thing. There *wasn't* much time to make a decision as to where Bekki's new life would go next. In a few weeks' time, she would potentially be homeless. Or even worse, she could be moving back in with her mum and dad.

At this point in the journey, the middle section of Notebook Number Two got filled up with all sorts of lists - 'to-do' ones and 'wish' ones - plus budgets and figures and plans for the future, things to get rid of and things to keep.

There was only one short letter and its response during this time:

Dear Alice,
I want everything to change, I really do. But it's

*all happening very quickly. I'm scared. It's hard to
do this on my own.*

> *Love,*
> *Bekki (and Rebecca) x*

Dear Girls,

> *The thought of change is always scarier than the
> change itself. All the things that can happen, and all
> the things that might happen, exist first and loom
> largest in our thoughts. Once change has happened,
> most of these thoughts will evaporate because reality
> is much smaller than imagination and all the things
> that might have been won't have happened.*

> *Alice x*

After these letters, the lists and plans became more
focussed and realistic. Moving out of the city she'd lived in
all her life was naturally scary for Bekki, but it was exciting
as well. The world was her oyster, within her budget, and
she quickly became addicted to house listings' websites
and estate agent's windows. It was a free and innocent type
of voyeurism. Property porn, if you will. As she window-
shopped for hours on end, she remembered her promise
to reduce judgement and criticism, although it had
slipped down from one percent to half a percent. 'Who
still has an avocado bathroom suite?' 'Not another 'Wine
o'clock' fridge magnet!' 'That's not a third bedroom, it's a
cupboard with a window,' and other such challenges to her
personal development.

It was all rather overwhelming. The more Bekki
searched, the more confused she got. She would have to

narrow it down. She remembered the advice from the posh sort with the flowery dresses on that TV show: 'The three most important words when house-hunting are location, location, location.' And so, Bekki accepted that of most importance was to decide where she wanted to be.

One Wednesday morning, with only a few weeks until the completion date on her flat and with her savings dwindling in her ISA, Bekki had a brainwave. She would go to the place where the decision to change her life had begun. Suffolk. It was only an hour and a half from London so she could go and explore the area and be back the same day. Several phone calls to estate agents later - why are most of them called Simon? - and five viewings were secured for later that week.

Apart from the fateful break to the holiday cottage just a few months before, Bekki had never been to Suffolk. She didn't know anyone who lived there or how easy it might be to find paid employment that she was suited to. In fact, until that first visit to the county, she had thought that Suffolk was in Cornwall.

Bekki had done a little research of her own before booking appointments, and decided it would be practical to be somewhere near a mainline train station and a regular supply of cappuccinos. She wasn't yet ready for self-sufficiency and so these things were non-negotiable. This narrowed her search to quaint-sounding towns like Haverhill and Ipswich. When she looked back through her emails, she discovered that she had had her original epiphany in a small village just outside Stowmarket, so that was the area she was going to check out first.

Rural estate agents are really no different to urban

ones. They may talk a little slower, as a general rule, but they all speak the same language. When they say 'low maintenance garden' they mean a concrete back yard the size of a bus stop. 'Character property' means old and damp with possible woodworm and planning restrictions. 'Good road links' means next to the bypass, so don't even think about getting a cat. And, as previously mentioned, they are mostly called Simon.

The early autumn sun was shining bright in Suffolk when Bekki pulled up outside the offices of Pottage & Lovett Estate Agents in Bury St Edmunds. This is mostly a pretty town with narrow streets and an abundance of hanging baskets. All the rough bits are tucked behind shops or pushed out to the edges by the dual carriageway. The estate agent's office was right in the heart of the town where the pretty bits were. Simon was waiting for her inside the office, cradling a caramel latte. He was relieved that the sun was shining as it would improve at least one of the properties he was planning to show his potential client from the big city. Bekki was relieved to see that it was possible to find caramel lattes so far from Islington. Her budget was miniscule in London, but in Suffolk she had just enough for a small cottage with its own garden. By moving out of the capital, she would finally be able to afford her own stairs.

The Suffolk countryside, on the best of days, is softly romantic. The green and pleasant landscape of John Constable, punctuated by small market towns and villages, is the embodiment of glorious Middle England, as referred to in Conservative Party manifestos. If a haywain suddenly popped out from behind a bush, nobody would bat an eyelid. Despite boasting at least one cathedral, Suffolk is the only county in England that doesn't contain a city. Those who are sensitive enough can feel the lack of a heaving metropolis and all that would be thrust out and soiled around it.

As Simon drove Bekki around the green-lined A-roads in his logo-festooned Skoda, she took the time to gaze out of the window and breathe it all in. She imagined herself planting raised vegetable beds made from railway sleeper and browsing farmers' markets with handmade linen shopping bags over her shoulder. She wasn't listening as Simon regaled her with tales of market increases and sealed bids. She simply said, 'really?' in convenient gaps in his monologue. Simon didn't notice. As soon as he felt a client on the end of his line, his conversation was like his driving - too fast and oblivious to anyone around him. Fortunately, Bekki was able to tune him out like a community radio station. Her thoughts were on the future. She had a good feeling about it.

In all, Simon showed Bekki around seven properties in two hours. Five that she'd originally requested to view, and two that had been on his books for over a year, 'just waiting for someone with vision.' The various villages had all blurred into one, and by the third property, Bekki had no idea if they were still in the same county. Simon assured her that all of them were within easy reach of good transport links, which did not mean the same as it did in London. What it actually means, in most of Britain's rural areas, is that there's a bus within a twenty-minute walk that ceases at six o'clock with no service on Sundays and Bank Holidays. If you were lucky, that bus stopped somewhere you wanted to go without having to change three times or walk the last four miles. As for rural taxis, it was cheaper to buy a horse and a paddock to keep it in.

All of the houses within Bekki's budget were on the small side but wildly different. There was a chocolate-box thatched cottage with pink walls that needed a new bathroom, kitchen floor, and mains electricity supply; there were two ex-council houses with handkerchief-sized gardens overlooked by several neighbours and a pylon; there was a new-build with en-suite wet room conveniently located next to an Olympic-sized Tesco car park; and a pair of semi-detached barn conversions down a farm track, sold individually or together, that were, according to Simon, 'a rare investment opportunity.' All of these paled into insignificance as they pulled up outside house number seven.

Before Bekki had even got out of the car, she knew deep down that this was the house for her. Like all sharp estate agents, Simon recognised the smell of a sale in the bag. His nostrils were filled with the heady aroma as he fished inside his faux-leather briefcase for the keys.

Bluebell Cottage was a two-bedroom, end of terrace, with a pretty garden backing onto open fields. It was in a reasonably-sized village with 'good local amenities,' which meant it had an overpriced corner shop, a disused phone box, one bus stop, and a pub. There was also a village hall, and a skate park that had been closed to children for three years because they made too much noise when they used it and the neighbours had complained. It was also just a few miles outside Stowmarket, which fitted perfectly into the map inside Bekki's head. Direct trains to London from there ran regularly, even on Sundays and Bank Holidays.

Simon's voice changed as he opened the front door and led Bekki around the cottage. He dropped his tone to a warm, friendly, almost paternal way of speaking. He knew that he had her. Now was the time to sit back and let her come to him. He needn't have bothered trying at all. Bekki was in love. She even liked the curtains - thick, linen drapes embroidered with cornflowers and bumble bees.

'The bathroom is downstairs,' Simon cooed, 'but that's quite normal for a property of this age. People are used to it round here. It means that the bedrooms upstairs are both doubles, and it's always handy to have a downstairs loo, am I right?'

'Really,' said Bekki, not paying attention in the slightest.

'And the windows are single-glazed, which you might have spotted, but it's a very quiet location. It also keeps the house nice and cool in the summer months. Double glazing is always an option, of course, and you'll want to put your own stamp on the place anyway.'

'Sure.'

'And it's not listed or anything, so you can pretty much do what you like, if you have the vision, and I think that you do. Subject to planning permission, of course.'

'Really.'

'No doubt. And oil-fired central heating means no gas bills, which is a bonus. Did I mention that the village pub has four rosettes for scampi? And the community-run shop is…'

Bekki was ready. She didn't want to wait any more. She interrupted before Simon could tell her exactly what the community-run shop was. Bekki couldn't care less. 'How much?' she asked.

'Well, I do need to tell you - and I wouldn't normally do this - but I've got two more viewings on this one tomorrow. Of course, if I get an offer today...'

'How much?'

'And there's no onward chain because the previous owner recently passed away in a tragic tombola accident at the village fair, which is an annual event, by the way. The fair, I mean, not the accident.' Simon snorted a laugh that bounced around the room.

Bekki snatched the property details from Simon's sweaty hands and scanned the front page, trying hard to focus on her head rather than her heart as she searched for the price. Simon opened his mouth to add more ammo to his argument, but Bekki stopped him before he could reload. 'I'll offer ten thousand under the asking price. The sale of my flat in London is almost complete so I can move quickly.'

'Ten thousand, you say? Well, I have to put your offer forward...'

'Subject to survey. I noticed some damp beside the wainscoting.' Bekki was finding a kind of courage that she had never known before. She also wasn't exactly sure what wainscoting was, but she had heard the woman on the telly with the flowery dress talk about them in character properties such as these.

Simon was a pro. He'd had two weeks' training in Tostock before they let him out on his own. He knew how to keep his head. 'Would you like to have one more look around? The toilet is only six months' old, and the flooring in the kitchen is vintage quilted lino. Very on trend.'

111

'I'll give you nine and a half under the asking price if I can keep the curtains.' Bekki had no formal training in house-buying.

'Let me make the call. I like good houses to go to good people. I'm just going to pop out to the Skoda to get a signal. Feel free to have a walk around the garden while I'm gone. There's a lovely sculpted heron by the oil tank.'

Simon tried very hard not to skip out of the door like a nineteen-fifties schoolgirl in case any of the neighbours saw. The grown-up nephew and last surviving descendant of the unfortunate tombola victim would be ecstatic to be offered over fifteen thousand pounds more than the house was actually worth. Pottage & Lovett had been pushing their luck with the asking price, which was probably why they'd had the house on their books for so long. The nephew was waiting greedily for the proceeds of his dear old uncle's estate so that he could finally afford to divorce his wife and convert his garage into a neo-Georgian garden pub with working pumps. He hadn't visited his uncle in years.

The back garden of Bluebell Cottage had clearly been loved once, but that had been some time ago. Roses and bindweed and dandelions now shared borders around a rectangular lawn-turned-meadow. A meandering, overgrown row of grey stepping stones led to a large wooden shed at the bottom of the garden that Bekki didn't notice until she was stood right in front of it. She carefully pulled back the brambles that hid the windows and peered inside. It was full of dusty old tools and paint tins but a good size and solidly built with a red slate roof. *This will be a perfect spot for writing in my notebooks,* she thought.

This property just kept getting better. Ignoring the fact that she'd never done a day's weeding in her life and had killed every houseplant she'd ever been bought as a gift, Bekki fantasised about creating the perfect cottage garden. *A swing seat over there, a water feature in the middle, and maybe a seated Buddha by the shed. Lovely,* she thought.

Simon strode out into the garden, waggling his mobile phone towards Bekki and beaming like a plumber on pay day. 'Congratulations, Miss Reeves. Bluebell Cottage is yours.'

Bekki tried to play it cool, but she was dancing and whooping on the inside. 'Will they leave the curtains and the shed?'

'The curtains, the shed, and the Stannah stairlift.'

Back in London, Bekki spread the printed details of Bluebell Cottage that Simon had left with her on the coffee table. She gazed at the colour photos of her soon-to-be-home. The stripped pine kitchen units and the blue and white tiles. The double-aspect master bedroom with stripped floorboards and loft access overlooking the garden. The sunlit, South-facing living room with the brick inglenook fireplace, 'not currently in use.' The Stannah stairlift - she'd have to get rid of that.

Bekki thought that she should call her mother to break the good news that she wouldn't be homeless once her flat sale went through. Then the bad news that she was moving further away from her parents. At least, it would be bad news for her mother. Bekki was delighted about that particular aspect of her new life. But first, and while she was still in a good mood, she wrote a letter to Alice.

Dear Alice,

Soon I will have a new home. It's PERFECT, or it will be when I've finished with it. Now it feels like I can really start to live the life that I want! I will write again soon, but first I have a lot of packing to do.

Buzzing with excitement,
Bekki xx

Alice didn't reply straight away. She knew that Bekki was on a high, and there's no point in reasoning with a person when they are either very high or very low. Neither of those states are entirely rational. Alice cared deeply about Bekki, so she waited until the morning to say something to her through the notebook.

Dear Bekki,

I'm very happy for you. I hope you had a good sleep as you have much to do and will need lots of energy to do it.

There are two things that I think you need to remember:

1. You do not need an excuse to start the life that you want. It began when you took your first breath. Everything you have lived has led you to now, and everything you live today will build tomorrow.

2. Perfection is the aspiration of the deluded. Don't waste your time on it.

Good luck, and see you in Suffolk.
Alice.

Chapter 11

One Earth (Peace) Ltd were the organisers of the Mind, Body & Spirit Fair that took place in a community centre in Kilburn every year. Bekki had never been to that kind of event before, but her sister Jane was a regular attendee. There was one happening that very weekend, and she insisted that Bekki went with her before moving out of London. The sisters had had a couple of conversations about Bekki's plans and ideas, such as they were, and Bekki had thought Jane really wasn't interested. Every time she'd brought the subject up, it had felt like a total waste of time. At best Jane's eyes would glaze over, and at worst she just laughed in her face.

Despite the fact that the sisters were never going to be kindred spirits, Bekki loved Jane and thought it might be nice to spend a day with her, wherever they were going. She couldn't imagine her sibling popping down to Suffolk on a regular basis and she was going to miss her.

Outside the community centre turned Temple of Tranquillity, a young blonde woman in dungarees smiled and thrust a piece of paper into Bekki's hands. 'Welcome,' she said. 'There's three pounds off rebirthing in the refectory today. Show them this leaflet for a discount. Enjoy.'

Jane and Bekki entered the hut and were guided to a

cloakroom where they could leave their coats for a small donation to an Ashram in Epping. 'What the hell are we doing here, Jane?'

'Shhh! Don't say 'hell' in here. You might upset a druid or something,' and Jane laughed so hard at her own joke that a small tear leaked out of the outer corner of her eye and smudged her mascara.

'Very funny. You've had your laugh. Why did you bring me here?'

'Well, I figured that you think you're on some kind of journey of development, Bekks, so I thought...'

'I don't think, I *know*,' interrupted Bekki, a little disgruntled.

'Whatever. The point is, you don't really know what you're doing, but you think it's 'spiritual' or something, don't you?' Jane made little quote marks in the air with her fingers around the word 'spiritual.' Bekki hated it when people did that.

'I don't know if it's spiritual or philosophical or even crazy. I just know that it's right.'

Whatever Jane's personal views on the meaning and purpose of life, she could see that her big sister was genuinely searching for something. Deep down she was happy for her. 'Let's go with what you said, right? Whatever it is that's got you all weird, it's a bit of challenge for you at the moment. Is that fair?'

Bekki nodded. 'I suppose so.'

'Well, this place is full of weirdos who have been doing this for longer than you, so I thought you might find a bit of guidance or something. You've got to have an open mind, though.'

'How very dare you!' Bekki landed a playful slap on Jane's left arm. 'My mind *is* open, which is more than I can say for yours. And how do you know about these people anyway?'

'I come to this fair every year. I'm a regular.' Just to prove the point, Jane handed her Puffa jacket to the middle-aged, barefoot man inside the cloakroom, plus a pound for the Epping Ashram. 'Wotcha Centaur. How's the kids?'

'Hi Janey. Everyone's hunky dory. How's yourself?'

'Oh, you know, one step ahead of the law and two steps ahead of fashion.'

'Good to hear it,' said the man, hanging up a midnight blue, crushed velvet cape as he spoke. 'Catch you on the other side.'

Bekki was astonished at the familiarity. She handed her own quite boring jacket to Centaur and followed her sister out of the cloakroom. 'You really have been here before.'

'I just told you,' said Jane over her shoulder as she walked on towards the main hall, 'I come every year. Not just here, but other MBS fairs too.'

'But why?' Bekki persisted. 'I didn't think you believed in any of this stuff.'

'I don't really,' shrugged Jane. 'I come for the henna tattoos and the jewellery. Moonstones as big as your fist for a tenner. These people have no idea how much things cost in the real world. You know that opal ring set in a dragon's claw that I've got? I bought it right here last year for fifteen pounds. Sterling silver too. Gotta be worth at least fifty.'

'Well, that makes more sense.'

'The people are generally nicer than the ones you find down the pub, too, and a bit more honest. I reckon they're all scared of being reincarnated as a slug or something. Check it out. What do you think?'

The main hall of the community centre was lit by the late winter sun streaming in through the large windows all along three sides of the room. It was busy with punters of all ages. An overwhelming aroma of patchouli oil and lavender hit the sisters when they opened the door and walked in. The ceiling of the room was high and vaulted and the buzz of chatter around the numerous tables filled the hall like the hum of restless wasps. Trestle tables covered with a rainbow of tablecloths lined the walls and ran down the centre of the space. Behind each one was a purveyor of new age knowledge of one kind or another: tarot readers, Reiki healers, incense sellers, digital-age astrologers with laptops, aura artists, crystal dowsers, palmists, and to the delight of Jane, vendors of all kinds of jewellery and accessories.

'Ooh! Toe rings!' yelped Jane with glee. 'You have a mooch around while I check out the sparkly stuff.'

'Where do I start?' Bekki felt a little overwhelmed. She wasn't closed to the idea of trying new things, she just didn't expect to find so many of them all in one room.

'Just have a wander,' encouraged Jane. 'Maybe have a reading or something. I'll meet you in the tea room in half an hour.' And she pushed her sister in one direction while she went in the other to make a beeline for a table dripping with silver nose studs and dragon pendants.

The first table that Bekki passed was that of an aura

artist called Bob. She was expecting everyone at the fair to be called Eagle or Sun Spirit but, according to the calligraphy sign on the table, he was just plain 'Bob: Spirit Artist. Have your aura drawn. £10 or two for £15.' He was busy sketching something ethereal with blue and yellow chalks and didn't look up from his work, totally engrossed in something invisible to everyone else.

At the next table was a palmist in the middle of a reading for a middle-aged woman with two bags of heavy shopping at her feet and a small, sleeping dog on her lap. The palmist was called Stella, according to her table sign, and the two women were deep in conversation in hushed tones, heads almost together across the table. Stella was holding the woman's hand and nodding sagely. There was a piece of paper next to the palmist's sign were people could sign up for the next available slot. Bekki glanced at it. There wasn't a space for another two and a half hours. *Maybe Stella's good,* thought Bekki, but she didn't stop to add her name to the list.

Bekki walked past the next few tables quite briskly, mostly because she didn't know what Reiki was and didn't want to discuss her chakras with the man who had the diagrams. In any case, she didn't know what chakras were either.

In the centre of the room was a row of tables with a little more space around them, and here were the practitioners and therapists. One man was snoring loudly in a reclining chair, clearly more than relaxed from his Indian head massage. Nobody tried to wake him. Another was having his aura cleansed by a lady in a white kimono, while an elderly woman sat smiling serenely as a much younger woman performed shiatsu massage on her tired-looking feet. As Bekki watched with growing curiosity, she heard the young shiatsu woman say: 'We're going to have to remove that corn plaster so that we can get to your evacuation zone, Mrs Ambrose.' At that point, Bekki decided to move on to the other side of the room.

Jane was still at the first jewellery stall attempting to make a deal with the vendor on a bulk purchase. Bekki decided to leave her to it and make her way over to a smaller ante-room in the corner where she could see that teas and coffees and vegan delicacies were available. She walked past the rest of the tables at a speed that she deemed to be the most respectful, glancing at the offerings and trying not to look too out of place.

Before she could reach some much-needed coffee, somebody caught her eye. Sitting back in a chair behind the last-but-one table before the tea room was a small woman with large hair, probably around Bekki's own age. Her stall was draped in a green and yellow cloth that hung to the floor. On it was a sign that said: 'Carrie Fisher. Psychic Readings: £6 for 15 minutes.' The only other thing on the table was a diamond-shaped pink crystal, not too big but glinting in the light that came in from the window opposite.

Carrie Fisher smiled at Bekki but made no movement to entice her in. The chair in front of the table was empty, and before she realised what she was doing, Bekki sat down in it. 'Hello,' said Carrie. 'Would you like a reading? I don't have another appointment for half an hour, so I could do you now, if you like.'

'Is that your real name? Carrie Fisher?' said Bekki. She

didn't know how to start a conversation with a psychic and was grateful for anything she could grab hold of.

'Yes, I'm afraid it is,' said Carrie Fisher.

'You don't look anything like Princess Leia!' Bekki snorted a laugh and felt her cheeks get hot with stupidity.

'That's the first time anyone's ever said that to me,' said Carrie Fisher.

'Really?'

'No,' said Carrie Fisher.

'Sorry. I've never been to one of these fairs before. I'm not sure what you're supposed to do.'

'I could tell,' said Carrie. 'I've been watching you move around the room. I'm very pleased that you sat down.'

'Are you?' Bekki's natural curiosity was aroused. 'Why?'

'Because you looked lost, and a teeny bit scared.'

'I am. In more ways than one.' Bekki took a deep breath and relaxed into her chair a little. She glanced over her shoulder, looking for her sister. She'd moved along a couple of stalls and was busy browsing a large display of silver pendants. She'd be there for a while. 'Okay,' said Bekki. 'I'd like a reading please. Do I cross your palm with six pounds first?'

Carrie Fisher gave a soft little laugh. 'No, it's okay. We're not all Madame Arcati. You can pay me after the reading, if you feel it's been worth your while.'

'Okay, that's fair.' Bekki put her bag down on the floor between her feet and relaxed a bit more. 'What do I have to do?'

'First you can tell me your name,' said Carrie.

'You can call me Bekki.'

'Okay, Bekki. If you're ready to start, I'm just going to close my eyes for a moment and try to home in on your spirit guides.'

Bekki was pleased that Carrie Fisher couldn't see her as she was trying her best to stifle a laugh, especially if her sister happened to be watching. Then she remembered that she was trying to reduce criticism in her life, so she pulled herself together and decided to reserve judgement and give Carrie Fisher a chance. It was a couple of minutes before the psychic spoke again. In that time, Bekki noticed that the background drone of voices around the room seemed to fade into the distance more and more and more, as if somebody was turning down the volume. It was very curious.

Carrie reached out to pick up the pink crystal from the table. Her eyes were still closed but her hand found it easily. She placed it in her palm and wrapped her fingers around it tightly. Then she opened her eyes, leaned in towards the table and spoke in a clear, soft voice. It was not much louder than a whisper but Bekki could hear the words quite easily as the noise of the room now seemed to disappear entirely. 'They're saying that they want to speak to Alice.'

'Who? What? Erm...' Bekki was taken aback at this opening gambit. 'I don't know anybody called Alice,' she said, reasoning to herself that it was not quite a lie but a half truth.

'Never mind. They're telling me to talk to you just the same.' Carrie Fisher paused to take a deep breath. She let the air back out slowly through half-closed lips. 'So, you've found your path,' said Carrie, 'and you've decided to follow it wherever it takes you.'

'Okay,' said Bekki, but she was a little disappointed. The reading had started so impressively specific, but the follow up could be interpreted in a million different ways. *Don't judge yet,* she reminded herself, and decided to listen with a bit more patience.

'It's a long journey,' continued Carrie, 'and you've decided to begin it on your own. That's a lonely choice. Did you think that others wouldn't understand it? Your mother might not, but there are some true friends around you.'

Bekki shrugged.

'Never mind,' said Carrie. 'You won't always be travelling alone. Best not to be closed to sharing the journey.'

Despite her misgivings, Bekki responded quite honestly. 'My friends and family don't understand. I tried to explain and it fell on deaf ears, or else they just laughed. They were nice about it, but they laughed all the same.'

'That's because you told them without showing them.'

'What do you mean?' Bekki frowned. The conversation was getting very deep very fast.

'It's still early days for you. Ideas are swifter than actions, and your intentions are not yet realised. They will be. Everything's changing very quickly in your life, and because you're moving so fast, it can look like everything else is standing still, but it isn't. I know it can be frustrating, but that will pass. Does any of this make sense?'

Bekki nodded.

'Take a while to catch up with yourself. When you get to Suffolk, take some time out to get used to your new life, and it will take more time than you wish, but that's the way of these things.'

'How do you know I'm moving to Suffolk?' Bekki was a tad alarmed at the accuracy of Carrie's last statement. She was expecting to be told that she was going to take a holiday in the future and to look out for tall, dark strangers and the number eight. This was surprisingly specific.

'Did I say Suffolk?' asked Carrie.

'Yes, you did.'

'Oh, well. Half the time I don't even hear what's coming out of my mouth. It's the spirits, not me. I try not to interfere.'

'You don't know my sister, Jane, by any chance?' Bekki pointed over to Jane, who was now having the back of her hands tattooed with Henna at one of the stalls in the middle of the room.

Carrie glanced over at Jane. 'No, I don't think so. This is my first time at this particular fair. I live down in Cornwall. Do you think your sister might like to join us?'

Bekki shook her head. She believed that Carrie was telling the truth. Jane was the kind of person who was once met, forever remembered. 'Can I ask you a question?' she said.

'Yes, of course,' said Carrie. She put the pink crystal back on to the table, giving it a little stroke as she did so, then she leaned back in her chair and rested her hands in her lap.

'Are there really spirit guides looking after me?' asked Bekki.

'Yes, there are. At least three, as far as I can tell.'

'Three?'

'Yep. I can only see one of them clearly. He looks oriental, and quite old. The other two are a bit blurry.'

'I'm sorry, but I'm not sure that I believe in spirit guides.'

'Does it matter?' The psychic said this with no trace of challenge or expectation and followed it with a smile. It was a genuine question.

Bekki thought about it for a moment, then answered as sincerely as she could. 'I don't suppose it does. Do *you* believe that there are spirit people talking to you about me? That these things are real?'

Carrie shrugged and smiled again. 'I honestly don't know. All I do know is that people come and sit with me and a sort of bubble of peace descends upon us. Have you noticed how quiet the room became when we started speaking?'

'Yes,' said Bekki, 'I did. That's amazing. Did you notice it too? I thought I was imagining it.'

'No, you weren't. I heard it. That's how all my readings start. I'm always astonished when it happens. It's like something is telling me to get ready to begin, and I listen. Not everybody notices it, but you did. And then, once the volume of our surroundings has dropped to a hush, words and pictures just pop into my head and I pass the messages on. I don't know how it works, it just does. And if people feel that there's been nothing in it, then I don't charge them. They usually pay, though.'

'You see pictures too?'

'Yes, but they don't always make sense so I don't always mention them. This isn't an exact science, you know. It's a natural thing. Not every seed you plant in the ground comes up as a flower. Any gardener can tell you that.'

'Have you seen anything around me since I've been sat

down?' Bekki was increasingly intrigued and warming to the woman. She felt nothing but genuineness and warmth from her.

'I did see something, actually, but I couldn't fit it to you so I didn't say it out loud.'

'What was it?'

'It was hordes of zombies being beheaded on some kind of screen. I must have fallen asleep in front of the telly last night. But that wasn't your real question, was it? You haven't asked your real question yet.'

'I guess not,' admitted Bekki.

'You've been answering your own questions, haven't you?' said Carrie. 'What you really want to know is whether the answers you've been receiving are true or not.'

'Yes,' said Bekki. 'I don't even know how I'm answering them. They just come out of nowhere and I write them down. Where are they coming from?'

'I can tell you,' said Carrie. 'They're coming from the parts of you that normally have to be silent.'

'What do you mean?'

'We all have parts of us that know better than we do in our everyday lives. They have wisdom that is ancient and in our genes, passed down from generation to generation. It's a type of instinct, like how we all have the urge to walk as infants, even if nobody shows us how. It's just that most people don't listen to these parts and so they remain silent. Even worse, people are persuaded that what is unnatural is normal and what is natural is worthless. It's a sad state of affairs.'

'Are you saying that I'm just talking to myself?'

'Yes and no. Some of it is the future you; the one that you're hoping to become one day.'

'Alice.' Bekki blurted out the name and then pressed her lips together tightly. She'd only met this person with the unlikely name a few minutes ago and she was revealing more of her secrets to her than she cared to share even with her sister.

'So, you *do* know someone called Alice. No, wait,' Carrie paused to get her words in the right order. She tilted her head to one side, as if she was listening to a voice in her ear. 'Alice said it's safe to mention her name here. She also said that not all of her messages are answers. Some are pointers and some things she'll need to think about for longer before she gets back to you.'

Bekki shifted in her chair a little self-consciously. 'Can you see Alice?'

'Yes, I can,' said Carrie. 'I see her as clearly as I see you right now.'

'Sorry,' said Bekki. 'I should have told you that I do know someone called Alice.'

'It's okay,' said Carrie Fisher. 'Take-off and landing are the most difficult and dangerous parts of any journey. Once you get up to a higher altitude, you can take your time and enjoy the in-flight movie before you have to come back down to earth. You'll make lots of these trips as you go on. Just remember to put on your eye mask and take a nap once in a while. Is there anything else? Our time is nearly up.'

'Yes,' said Bekki. 'Just one quick thing. How do I know what is truth and what isn't?'

'That's easy,' said Carrie, not fazed by the question at all. 'The truth can be found everywhere and in everything around you. The problem is that every truth today sits next to a million lies. The trick is not to chase the truth in the first instance, but to avoid as many lies as you can. The more you practise, the more truth you'll come across. Anything else?'

'Yes, lots,' said Bekki.

'Maybe we'll meet again sometime,' said Carrie Fisher. 'I'll give you one of my cards in case you want to talk some more over the phone.'

As the psychic reached into her bag under the table for a business card, Bekki reached for her own bag to fetch her purse. She got out six pound coins and put them on the table. 'Thank you,' she said. 'I'm happy to pay you.'

'I'm glad it was your worth your while,' said Carrie. She took the coins and handed her card to Bekki. It was a plain, turquoise card with just her name and a phone number on it. Bekki slipped it into her bag and the two women said their goodbyes.

As Bekki ordered herself a soya frappuccino with nutmeg sprinkles, Jane appeared at her side. Both of her hands and one temple were now emblazoned with curly henna pictograms, and a collection of new jewellery was clinking in a variety of small paper bags slung over her wrist. 'Get us a can of full fat Coke sis,' said Jane. 'I'm absolutely gagging.'

'Sorry,' said the woman behind the counter. 'We don't sell *Coke*,' and she spat the brand name out of her mouth like she'd accidentally swallowed a cow pat. 'I can do you an elderflower and rhubarb pressé, if you like. I bottled it myself.'

'That will do,' said Jane.

The sisters sat and drank and talked as Kilburn's One

Earth Mind, Body & Spirit Fair swirled around them. They laughed and shared stories and Bekki felt relaxed in Jane's company, which didn't happen that often. She told her about the reading, and her sister didn't laugh as much as she expected her to.

Bekki kept Carrie Fisher's card. She pasted it inside the back cover of Notebook Number Two. She never did call to ask her more questions. In truth, the psychic had told her all she needed to know.

Later that night, sitting in her living room in Islington among the packing boxes and suitcases, Bekki sat down to write a short letter in Notebook Number Two.

Dear Alice,

It was an interesting day. I met a psychic who told me things I knew and a couple of things I didn't know. I haven't quite made up my mind about whether or not I believe in telepathy and clairvoyance and all that, but I did believe in her.

I'm going to take a little time out for myself tomorrow and just think about everything that's happening. I'll write again soon.

Love,
Bekki xx

There was an even shorter reply in Alice's best handwriting.

Dear Bekki,
I liked her too. Rest well.
Alice x

Chapter 12

Alice didn't hear from Bekki again until she'd moved out of London and into her new home in Suffolk. In other words, there was only one further correspondence between them in Notebook Number Two. By then it was March. All the plants and the trees were ready to leap out of their winter beds and start their annual rampage. Instead of letters, Notebook Number Two had been filled up with 'to do' lists, contact numbers of solicitors and removal firms, plans for various rooms with diagrams, pictures cut from magazines of shabby chic furniture and 'ideal' homes, running totals of expenditure and dream shopping lists, and all kinds of other goals that people record for themselves in an attempt to move them one step closer to reality.

As a small aside, Bekki discovered at this time that, in the same way that all estate agents are called Simon, it was also true that all builders over forty are called Lee. All those under forty are called Nick. This was the same whether a partition wall was required to be erected in Glasgow, Liverpool or Cardiff. This was a completely useless piece of information, but it did show that Bekki was beginning to observe the patterns in things. Most people hardly seem to notice.

Notebook Number Three was blank and ready to

receive, waiting for the next part of Bekki's journey to begin. The first piece of furniture she bought for the cottage was a small, white-painted bookcase. Today, an item like this would be called 'pre-loved.' Back then it was simply second-hand and a bargain. The white bookcase would be the future home for the notebooks, along with a few of the books on her 'to read before I die' list in Notebook Number Two. At the last time of checking, Bekki had read three of the fifty-six books on the list.

There is much to do in a new home, particularly one located in an unfamiliar place. And especially one that is old, as Bekki discovered when she lifted the lino in her quaint, blue and white kitchen. She would have to ask Lee down the road to investigate that crack in the floor and find out where that strange smell was coming from.

Summer came and went in a flash. Old wallpaper was replaced with fresh paint, rugs were bought, and pictures were accumulated and hung around the walls. Flowering shrubs that Bekki had never heard of were popping up all over her garden. Not being naturally green-fingered, she either left them alone or cut them back completely at random. For her birthday, Bekki's mother bought her a gardening book for beginners by ex-pop star, Kim Wilde, now an award-winning horticulturalist. *Who knew?* thought Bekki. She took it as a sign of encouragement. *If Kim Wilde can change her life so drastically, from Top of the Pops to the Royal Horticultural Society, then changing my little life should be a breeze,* she thought.

Sometimes change comes when we least expect it. On the eleventh of September that year, an event happened that was so big that news of it would ripple out around the planet like a breeze block in a duck pond.

Bekki was up in the spare bedroom when it happened, finally getting around to sorting out some boxes that were still not unpacked and had been under the bed since she'd moved in. She pulled out the first one, opened it, and was dismayed to discover that it was full of old paperwork that would no doubt be boring but time consuming to sort.

Just as Bekki was about to grab the first handful of old bank statements and bills, the doorbell rang. She skipped down the stairs, relieved to have an excuse to procrastinate. It was Mrs Sudley, her elderly neighbour from the cottage next door. She looked pale and her eyes were wide and alert as if she was in shock. 'Mrs Sudley, are you okay?' She'd never seen the old lady like this before. 'Is something wrong?'

'Have you got the telly on?' asked the neighbour.

'No,' said Bekki. 'I was sorting out some boxes upstairs. Was I making noise or something?'

'Come with me,' and the old lady grabbed Bekki's hand tightly and began to pull her out of the front door.

'Hang on,' said Bekki, pulling back her hand. The old lady had a surprisingly strong grip for her age. 'Just let me grab my keys,' and she turned to nip back inside to the kitchen to fetch them from behind the door.

'Have you got any biscuits?' called Mrs Sudley after her.

'I've got some chocolate digestives, I think,' called back Bekki from inside the house.

'Milk or plain?'

'Milk chocolate.'

'Good,' said Mrs Sudley. 'Bring those too.'

The old lady was clearly in some kind of distress and needed something sweet and crumbly. Bekki could help with that. She would be a good neighbour. She tucked the pack of biscuits under her arm as she locked the front door. Mrs Sudley was standing on the pavement, shifting her weight from foot to foot impatiently until Bekki was done and the front door was secured. 'Come on, come on,' she urged, as she led Bekki along the narrow pavement and in through her own open front door.

What sounded like the voice of a BBC newsreader on amphetamines was booming out from Mrs Sudley's kitchen, down the hallway and out through the front door. Bekki couldn't quite make out the commentary as she hurried behind the old lady, but the pictures that awaited her on the portable TV that sat on the pine Welsh dresser were a shock. They stopped her in her tracks. The animated tone of the newsreader's voice now made sense. All Bekki could say was, 'What the hell…?'

'Sit down,' said Mrs Sudley, directing Bekki towards one of the wooden chairs at the kitchen table facing the Welsh dresser. Bekki sat, staring at the TV screen, mouth open. 'Tea or coffee, dear?'

'Coffee,' said Bekki, as a kind of automatic response. Then, as an afterthought, 'Thank you.' In all situations, it's good to retain your manners. 'Is this live?' she asked.

'Yes. This is going on right now in New York where my cousin Aggie lives. I didn't want to watch it on my own,' explained Mrs Sudley. 'It felt historic, do you know what I mean?' She didn't wait for Bekki to reply. Her young neighbour's mouth was still open and her face looked stuck. The old lady put the kettle on and fetched a couple of mugs down from the dresser shelf, as if they shared a coffee in front of breaking news every day of the week. 'Where's the biscuits?' she asked.

'Here you go.' Bekki pushed the packet of biscuits across the table. Mrs Sudley fetched one of her best plates from the cupboard and arranged the milk chocolate digestives in a circular pattern. There might be a devastating, world-changing event unfolding live on the screen before their eyes, but that didn't mean one should drop standards of hospitality.

The two women drank coffee, ate biscuits, and sat together mostly in silence for a long time. They watched with a mixture of horror and curiosity, not knowing exactly what they should do or how they should be reacting, as live pictures of planes crashing into skyscrapers and people leaping from burning buildings were beamed into this and a billion other homes on the planet.

It was more than a couple of hours until Bekki returned home. Before she went, she made sure that her elderly neighbour was okay. She was fine. If anything, she was calmer than Bekki, and certainly more philosophical about the day's events. 'I was fifteen years old when my father was killed in the war,' she told Bekki over their third cup of coffee. 'Of course, they didn't show it live on the telly in those days, thank goodness.' And with that, Mrs Sudley consumed the last milk chocolate digestive and slipped the plate into the sink. The washing up could wait until tomorrow.

There were five messages on Bekki's answerphone when she got back indoors. Two were from her parents

- both speaking together on one message for a change - one from her sister, and a couple from old friends in London. They all said pretty much the same thing: 'Oh my God!' or 'Did you watch the news?' or 'I can't believe it!' and 'I don't know what to say,' and other such phrases of uncertainty in a crisis. There were also a few text messages from other friends and even a couple of old colleagues from Pitch Perfect Promotions, all with pretty much the same sentiment. It was as if people just needed to talk to each other; to say anything at all. Bekki decided she would return any calls that needed returning tomorrow. By then she might have thought of something to say herself.

When the next morning came, the phone was silent at both ends. Instead, Bekki turned to her notebooks in an attempt to say something that could make any kind of sense. Notebook Number Three was fresh and empty and waiting. She picked it up, ran her fingers over the unblemished cover, then put it down again. There were just a couple of pages left at the end of Notebook Number Two. It seemed fitting to write the following letter there so that she could close the book on it afterwards.

Dear... I don't know who to address this to. I think I just want to speak to somebody.

Yesterday was a very strange day. It all happened like I was watching a movie. It was real but far away. It was something almost alien. Or perhaps I was like an alien watching it.

After an initial sense of shock, the biggest thing I felt was powerlessness. There was nothing I could

do, so I just drank coffee and ate chocolate biscuits,
as if I was at the movies. It was so surreal.

I need some time to process all this. I need to
really think about it. I don't want to just be in shock
or react with hatred towards something I don't
understand. One thing I do know is that the world
changed forever yesterday. What does that mean? Is
it the beginning of something? Or is it the end?

Bekki xxx

The box of unsorted papers had been sat on the chest
of drawers in the spare bedroom since Mrs Sudley had
knocked on the door the previous day. Bekki closed the
open flaps on the top, picked up the box, and slid it back
under the bed. *It can wait,* she decided.

Alice also waited before replying to Bekki's letter. She
waited almost a week. In that time, there had been endless
news items and brand-new documentaries about the
event on TV, and several calls with her family, friends, and
neighbours. Everyone had an opinion. All were affected
by the events of the eleventh of September, in one way or
another. No doubt, there would be a movie sooner or later.

The letter from Alice appeared on the last page of
Notebook Number Two just at the point where Bekki
didn't think she could bear to hear anything else about the
now infamous incident.

It was late. Alice's letter was brief, so Bekki read it
straight away.

Dear Bekki and Rebecca,
Change comes in many forms, but come it will.

It always has. Every once in a while, the world appears to be ripped open in a sudden, violent way in order to facilitate a big change that needs to come. Whether that change is for the good of the human race or to its detriment is for each person to decide. We are all part of the same game. Meanwhile, many small changes are happening and hardly anybody notices.

This will be simpler one day when enough time has passed. Stay sane.

Alice.

That was one of the few letters that Alice wrote to Bekki and Rebecca at the same time. It felt comforting somehow. There had been times in the last week when Bekki had felt like a child in the face of everything. Maybe Rebecca was the little girl in her. It had been a testing time. She had felt naïve and helpless and nobody seemed to be able to soothe those emotions. Alice's letter helped.

Bekki read that letter three times more before going to bed. That night she slept for longer than she had slept in days.

And that was the end of Notebook Number Two. It was a big, dramatic 'full stop' to put at the end of one of the notebooks, but it was only the end of that particular one. There was much more still to write. There was much more still to discover. Tomorrow is always another day.

Chapter 13

Autumn hardly seemed to touch the sides of that year, and then the nights started drawing in. This was far more noticeable in the rural parts of Britain. Back in London, the street lights and tall buildings would shield people from the dark for longer.

It was now November and Bekki had discovered every draft and damp patch that Bluebell Cottage had been concealing when she'd moved in. She also discovered that oil-fuelled central heating was crap and very expensive, despite Simon the estate agent's insistence that it was 'the future.' After paying Lee the builder's bill for opening up the flue to the inglenook and installing a wood-burning stove, Bekki also discovered that wood burners and log fires were far more romantic in the movies than they were in real life. Nobody ever got covered in ash and poker blisters before making love on a sheepskin hearth rug in the movies. Not even in the old black and white ones, where you would expect to see at least see a few sooty fingerprints.

Bekki also discovered that her savings were almost gone, and she had nothing of value or general interest that she could sell on that new internet auction site that everyone was talking about. She might just get through Christmas in credit, but that would be it. It was time to go back into the world of paid employment. She knew it would come sooner or later. The latter would have been nice. She hadn't had to set a wake-up alarm in weeks. Her thoughts on this created the very first entry in Notebook Number Three. Not in the form of a letter, in this instance, so there was no reply from Alice or anybody else, although Bekki was now beginning to answer her own questions before they had a chance to.

13th November 2001, 11:45am

I'm here. And I'm lonely.

The cottage is coming together, and it's all mine - except for the mortgage. That bit belongs to the bank. I suppose I own one-and-a-half bedrooms, the kitchen and the bathroom. Oh, and the garden. Well, the shed, at least. I love the shade of blue on the bedroom walls, and I've finally got the hang of lighting the wood burner. It's messy, but it is warmer in the house now.

Did I mention that I'm lonely?

My next-door neighbour is nice. She's called Mrs Sudley and she's a widow in her seventies. She bakes all kinds of pies and brings me half. She says she used to bake for her husband, but since he died she's been throwing his half in the bin. I'm glad that she's not wasting food. She talks to me about her son and her cat and her dead husband, but I can't talk to her about the things I write in here. I mean, where would I start? How would it make her feel if I told her that everything about the world is a lie? That she had wasted her life baking pies and living vicariously through the men in her life? Or maybe she hasn't. Maybe it's me.

All of this makes me feel even more lonely. I need to find people I can really talk to. Not that Mrs Sudley isn't nice. She's lovely. So are her pies. She's human. Her pies are mostly apple and rhubarb.

I'm running out of money. Maybe that's why I'm a bit down right now. I need to find a job and soon. If I'm working with other people, I might not be so lonely. There must be somebody around here I can talk to. My old friends back in London seem very far away, and they're always busy. They think Suffolk is in Cornwall, like I used to.

Must-haves for new job:

Not too far away. Stowmarket or closer.

Working with other people, preferably below retirement age.

I can afford to work part-time, three or four days a week for life-work balance.

Nothing to do with advertising. This is a deal breaker.

I'm going to start job hunting tomorrow. There must at least be some seasonal Christmas work going. This new kind of existence is hard when you're trying to do it on your own. Searching for a purpose in life is lonelier than I expected it to be. Maybe that's why all those people join cults. At least they get to share a bedroom.

Bekki was true to her intentions. She didn't join a cult, but she did go job hunting. The very next morning she dressed in 'town clothes' and left the house. She'd been living in pyjama bottoms and sweatshirts for weeks, and it took a bit of manoeuvring before she felt comfy in a bra again. She drove into Stowmarket, determined to come home with at least the promise of employment. She thought it would be best to kick off with a coffee before walking round the whole town. It was a good move. As she entered *Tiffin Teas* near the car park, she spotted a sign in the window: '*VACANCY: Part-time café assistant required. Must be flexible, numerate and polite. Apply within.*' Surely it was fate. Although Bekki hadn't yet decided whether she believed in fate or not.

A fat brass bell on a spring jingled boisterously when Bekki pushed open the heavy glass door. It was busy inside the café, and noisier than the traffic and shoppers on the street outside. The black and white vinyl floor, the cream Formica tables and the large front windows bounced all the sound around the room, so that even the most hushed conversations could be eavesdropped on without strain. It all swirled into a tinny symphony, punctuated by percussion from the steam-frothing coffee machine and the dishes banging about in the kitchen that lay beyond the counter. There was a rough, Artex-covered archway between the two rooms where the customers could see through to the originator of all the background clinking of crockery.

A man was hunched over a long, stainless-steel sink, washing up as loudly as it was possible to without smashing the plates to pieces. He looked like he was in his fifties, or maybe in his eighties, depending on how deeply he frowned at any one time. Straight, thinning grey hair hung down to his shoulders with the side bits tucked behind his ears as if it naturally grew that way. His eyebrows grew out in thick clumps to his temples like they were trying to escape from his nose. This particular facial feature was alarmingly long and straight and thick and, even from a distance, a patch of fine, grey hairs could be seen languishing across the bridge of this eccentric snout.

Behind the café counter was a woman, just as hard to pin an age to as the man washing up in the kitchen, but she was definitely a little younger. She was of medium height but square-shaped with sinewy arms and big knuckles. As she wiped down the counter with a blue cloth, the muscles in her forearms stood proud like train tracks, strong and wiry from years of pushing those blue cloths around. Her hair was dyed raven black with little streaks of grey around the ears and crown where the dye hadn't quite reached, and it was all tied back in a high ponytail with a thick, red scrunchy to secure it away from her face and out of the food. She wore a pale grey apron printed with pink roses and looked completely at home in her surroundings. She was clearly the boss of the place. And if she wasn't, she should have been.

Bekki approached the counter with her best 'I'd like a job please' smile. On day one at Pitch Perfect Promotions she had learned from Uncle Julian that you can only make a first impression once, so she did her best to look friendly, intelligent, and highly numerate. 'Hello,' she said. 'I saw your notice in the window and...'

'What, love?' The lady behind the counter cupped a hand behind her left ear but carried on pushing the blue cloth across the counter with her other hand. She was so

143

good at it, she didn't even need to look at her hands but focused straight at the fake-smiling eyes of the awkward-looking young woman at the counter.

Bekki tried again a little louder. 'Hi, I saw the notice about the job in your window?' This was not a question but a statement. Bekki put a question mark at the end of it purely due to nerves. She hated it when other people did that. It always sounded so pretentious, unless you were Australian.

'Hang on a minute, I can't hear you.' The boss lady put down the blue cloth and turned to yell through the Artex archway. 'Oi! Alf! Keep it down in there. You're meant to be washing those cups not performing a drum solo!' She turned back around and spoke to the whole café. 'He thinks he's Ginger bloody Baker!' The customers who heard laughed or smiled. They were clearly used to this kind of banter.

Alfred - for that was the dishwasher's chosen name - dropped one more plate into the soapy sink with a deliberately loud splash, wiped his hands on his baggy brown t-shirt, and came out to face the woman behind the counter. Bekki saw then that his t-shirt was emblazoned with the slogan: 'If you want to get to heaven, you've got to ride like hell.' The words - possibly designed using the font *Lucida Blackletter*, which Bekki had seen used in many a German beer commercial at Pitch Perfect Promotions - encircled a picture of a silver Harley Davidson spitting flames out of its oversized exhaust. 'Alright, your highness,' said Alf to the boss lady. 'It's time for my break anyway.' He brushed no crumbs whatsoever from the spotless counter and settled his elbows down on it as close to the boss lady as he could without actually touching her. 'So, what's going on here then?' he said.

The boss lady rolled her eyes with a 'tut' then they both turned to the increasingly tense girl in front of them and waited for her to say something. Bekki paused for a moment, not sure who she was meant to be addressing, then decided that the woman must definitely be the boss because she hadn't been in the kitchen washing up. She flashed a desperate smile at her. Was it possible to make a first impression twice? She gave it a go. 'Hi,' she said once more. 'I saw your notice in the window and wondered if you were still looking for somebody because...'

'Why on earth would she advertise a job that doesn't exist?' interrupted Alf. 'Unless it's some kind of test for stupid people.' He grinned and his eyes twinkled with mischief. Or perhaps it was derision. Bekki couldn't be sure.

'Don't listen to him, love,' said the boss lady, 'he's on his break.'

Alf stood up straight, folded his arms and stared intently at Bekki, daring her to react. She didn't. At least, she did react, but only under her armpits. She hoped that nobody noticed that she was getting sweaty under there.

The boss lady sensed Bekki's discomfort. She folded up her blue cloth, tucked it under the counter, and softened her voice. 'Are you applying for the job, me dearie?' she said.

'Yes, I think so,' said Bekki. She wasn't altogether sure anymore. 'Can you tell me a bit more about it?'

'Well, I'm looking for someone for at least twenty hours a week, but you have to be flexible because the days

I need you will change depending on where I need to be. Are you flexible?'

'Yes, I am,' assured Bekki. 'I'm not working at the moment, so I'm free all the time.'

'That must be nice,' said Alf, folding his arms a little tighter across his chest. 'That's what we all want - freedom.'

'Ignore him,' said the boss lady. 'I'm Ruby and this is my café, not Alf's. He doesn't even work here.'

Bekki was confused at this piece of information but didn't like to ask. Alf just shrugged. 'I'm going out the back for a fag.' But he didn't go out the back at all. Instead, he took a battered tin out of the pocket of his jeans, opened it on the counter next to Ruby and proceeded to roll a skinny cigarette in liquorice paper. Ruby didn't appear to be concerned about the health and safety aspects of this in the slightest. Bekki waited to see if Alf would be daring enough to light a fag in a food preparation area. He didn't. He just stuck it between his teeth and waggled it up and down. Bekki hadn't smoked now for five months. She suddenly wanted a cigarette more than she had ever done in her life.

'My name's Bekki,' and then she didn't have a clue what she was meant to say next. She tore her eyes away from Alf's hypnotic cigarette with some difficulty, then smiled as confidently as she was able under the circumstances.

Thankfully, Ruby broke the spell. 'I need someone to start as soon as possible, dear, and I'll need some references from you before then.'

Getting back in touch with Julian at Pitch Perfect wasn't something Bekki was keen to do. In fact, she wasn't keen to even let them know that she'd changed her address since that business with the accidental severance pay. 'A reference from my last job might be a bit tricky,' she admitted.

'That's interesting information,' smirked Alf, finally taking the cigarette out of his teeth. 'Run off with the petty cash, did you, girlie?'

'No, no. Nothing like that.' Bekki blushed and couldn't hide it. 'It's just that I resigned on a matter of principle and left without working my months' notice.'

Ruby waved Bekki's blushes away with a flick of her hand. 'Don't worry about that, dear. It's nice to know you have principles. I never believe what people write in references anyway. Half of them are made up. Can you start on Tuesday? You'll be on probation for six months, which is better than a reference.'

'Six months? Is that normal for you?' said Bekki. That was longer than her probationary period at Pitch Perfect. It seemed like a long apprenticeship to clean tables and serve coffee.

'That's nothing,' said Alf. 'I've been here six years and I'm *still* on bloody probation.'

'Quit your noise,' said Ruby. 'I thought you were going out the back for a fag.' Alf bowed deeply with mock humility, turned with a flourish and disappeared through the kitchen and out the back door. 'So,' continued Ruby, 'do you want to give it a go, then?'

'Yes,' said Bekki. 'That would be great. What time do you want me to be here on Tuesday?'

'Half past eight,' said Ruby. 'Now, would you like a gingerbread latté while you're here? It's our winter special.'

'Yes, please,' said Bekki.

'Great, that will be one pound fifty.'

It wasn't until later that day when Bekki got home that she started to wonder whether *she* had got a job or a job had got *her*. Either way, she felt a great sense of relief. There would be wages coming in again. Bills could be paid and food could be bought without having to count the pennies so cautiously, and just in time for Christmas too.

She might even make some new friends at the café. That would be good. There must be a few younger people in Stowmarket. It was in this mood that Bekki wrote the first letter to Alice in Notebook Number Three. She used her favourite pen - one of those blue, felt tip ones that don't scratch the paper.

Dear Alice,

It's cold outside but it's a fine day indoors. In me, that is, and not inside the house, but I'm getting used to just putting an extra jumper on.

For the first time in weeks, the stress that comes with uncertainty has subsided enough to cause a flush of happiness. That's a little poetic for me, but that's just because I'm in a good mood.

I got a job today. It's only part-time but that suits me right now. I'm going to be working in a café in Stowmarket, the big market town nearby. It doesn't sound like much, but I've got a good feeling about it. Perhaps it's fate. Is there such a thing? Perhaps we create our own destiny, I'm not sure. Something feels right, all the same. I'll let you know how I get on.

Bekki xx

Alice responded, not straight away but a few hours later. She used the same blue pen. In that time, Bekki had eaten a large jacket potato with butter and cheese and drunk half a bottle of wine that she'd been saving for Christmas. Soon she'd be able to afford to replace it with something other than a Morrison's Merlot. Maybe even two bottles. She put the other half in the kitchen cupboard then got comfy on the sofa to read from her notebook.

Dear Bekki,

I'm very pleased to see you happy. Did you notice that there was a little bounce in the way you wrote that last letter? All the 'e's' look jolly and forward facing. You can tell a lot from a person's handwriting. That's why it's sad that so few people do it anymore. Some might even have forgotten how. All electronic messages look the same, but handwriting is an indicator of what a person feels and thinks, not just what they say. Try to notice it in yourself when you write to me. It will teach you a lot. Sometimes it's good to read backwards, but always remember to write forwards.

Good luck with the new job,
Alice

Bekki started at the café the following Tuesday. She got there fifteen minutes early so that she had time for a gingerbread latté first. They really were rather deliciously special. This time Ruby didn't ask her to pay for it. It was another small beginning in a whole chain of beginnings.

Bekki was optimistic.

Chapter 14

Things were going well for Bekki. Or at least they appeared to be. She was enjoying her job at the café and was grateful to have a boss like Ruby. If there was an antonym in the thesaurus for Julian at Pitch Perfect Promotions, it was Ruby at Tiffin Teas. She was even warming to Alf and his ways. She never went out the back for a cigarette on her breaks, although she was sorely tempted every time he did.

Bekki's financial worries had subsided a little, and she had enough income to live on for now. Surviving on a budget came naturally to her. It was in her genes. Her mother and grandmother had taught her well. They'd instilled old sayings into her like, 'Look after the pennies and the pounds will look after themselves,' and 'Neither a borrower nor a lender be.' It had worked. Bekki had always found a way to live within her means. Of course, this was now assisted greatly by the fact that her social life had shrunk by about ninety percent since moving from London to Suffolk. The lack of shoe shopping opportunities also helped.

Bluebell Cottage was feeling more and more like home. It was still draughty and impossible to heat, but her newly-acquired jumper collection was the envy of the village. Some acquaintances she'd recently made through the café had the potential to become more than that, and she might soon even count a couple of them as friends.

The festive season had come and gone leaving Bekki relatively unscathed. The Christmas day that she spent back at the old Reeves homestead was thankfully focused not on Bekki and her new, unconventional life decisions, but on her brother, who had been outed by Jane during the traditional pre-lunch gift giving. Her mother's initial shock turned to fury at being the last one in the family to know, and then to maternal pride at the thought of being a 'modern mum' at last. For the first time in Bekki's adult life, being in the presence of her mother did not illicit the words: 'Why can't you be more like your brother?' In fact, Mrs Reeves spent the whole of that season's James Bond movie phoning round her friends in the W.I. to rally support for a rainbow cake bake in January. The rest of the family could then relax and enjoy some spy-themed misogyny for Queen and country, while munching through two boxes of After Eights and a Terry's Chocolate Orange.

Some of Bekki's old London friends came to stay at the cottage for New Year's Eve. As is quite normal in the twenty-first century, she had lots of mates, but only a handful of true friends. These were the people in her life who could easily accept her faults and she theirs, and could be relied upon to pull her to safety in the event of her ever hanging off a cliff by her fingernails or dangling off a tree branch over a violent, swollen river. The exact number of these true friends was four, and three of them travelled to Suffolk to celebrate the new year in a very different way to how they celebrated the last.

Twelve months previously, all five friends had been in various states of nostalgic drunkenness at The Blind Womble in Cockfosters. The music was loud, the mojitos were salty, and by four o-clock in the morning they'd lost three shoes and one Oyster card between them. At Bluebell Cottage, it was a far more relaxed affair but the mojitos were just as salty, thanks to the mixing skills of Melissa Roley. She was Bekki's oldest friend, going all the way back to primary school where she was first christened with the imaginative nickname of 'Roley-Poley.' This had been a wild misnomer as she was a painfully thin child. The later shortening to 'Poley' - as she was known by all her intimates - worked much better. Standing at five foot eleven inches, and a svelte size ten, she did indeed resemble a pole.

The other two visitors were Phil and Bethany. She'd met them both at sixth form college when she had been forced by her mother to re-take her Maths A-level in order to secure some kind of future career that the neighbours might approve of. Phil now ran his own interior design business and Bethany worked for the Inland Revenue as a VAT specialist. Not bad for a couple of losers who failed Maths the first time around. The missing friend was Nathan, Phil's best friend. He was on tour in Canada playing rhythm guitar for a well-known Death Metal band, but texting regularly with tour bus gossip.

Midnight came and went. Mojitos were quaffed, hugs were shared, and old stories retold of when these nearly thirty-somethings were still young. In ten years' time, Bekki would look back at that first New Year's Eve in Bluebell Cottage and realise that at that age, they had in no way finished being young.

It had been a fun night. All four of them had snuggled down in sleeping bags, crowded around the living room floor. Mobile phones trilled with regular text messages from Nathan in Toronto throughout the night, and in Suffolk, one last bottle of Prosecco was popped open very, very late to celebrate midnight at the same time as him.

Everybody had loved Bluebell Cottage. It was twee and quiet compared to The Blind Womble. Even the lack of central heating seemed quaint. There were trees outside, no traffic noise, and the absence of emergency vehicle sirens was a novelty. After a late New Year's Day lunch at the local pub, it was time for everyone to head back home to London, well-fed and well-rested. The Hoof & Handcart up the road was no Blind Womble, but Simon the Estate Agent hadn't exaggerated about the scampi. Those four rosettes were thoroughly deserved. Everyone promised to come and visit Bekki again soon and there was lots of talk of 'let's all move to Suffolk where we can leave our phones unattended on pub tables.' But as designated driver Bethany pulled out of the pub car park, Bekki knew that 'soon' would probably mean months, and nobody else would ever move out of London, at least not until they retired or had children. She missed her old friends before the car was even out of sight.

Bluebell Cottage was quiet again. The living room was tidied and the empties were piled into the box behind the kitchen door for the bottle bank. As Bekki washed up the last of the dishes and drained the sink, the silence became unbearably loud. She began to feel very alone again. She questioned what on earth she was doing so far from the life she had always known. When her thoughts became too much, she made herself a big mug of hot chocolate, tipped in a good measure of Baileys, and settled down on the sofa. She switched on the TV and flicked through a few channels. There was nothing on that she wanted to watch. She tried her phone, but the mobile signal was down again. This was a regular occurrence whenever the rain was heavy, and it was bucketing down outside.

It had been over a month since Bekki had written in Notebook Number Three. New jobs and old friends and Christmas had been a welcome distraction in many ways, but now she missed her notebook. After a thorough search, she found it under a pile of clean washing in the bedroom. It was time to write another letter. She found a pen on the floor under the dressing table, and sat down on the bed to begin.

Dear Alice,

I don't know what to write, but I want to write something. I NEED to write something...

At this point, there was a pause in the letter. In that time, Bekki sat on the bed chewing the top of her pen. After a couple of seconds, she spat out a little ball of what she hoped was dust, wiped the pen on the underside of her pillowcase, then put it back in her mouth for the purposes of comfort and concentration. She continued chewing the top of the pen for a good fifteen minutes. Then she tucked the notebook under her arm and the pen behind her ear, and walked around the cottage, upstairs and down, for what seemed like hours. It was only about fifteen minutes. It was agony, all the same.

In the kitchen, she boiled the kettle to make another mug of hot chocolate, this time with an even more generous slug of Baileys added. She stirred the sickly-sweet liqueur into the even sweeter liquid chocolate and then tapped the spoon on the side of the mug. The sound echoed around the kitchen, bouncing off the tiles, piercing Bekki's brain like a number six knitting needle. Back in the living room, she settled down on the sofa and checked her phone again. Still no signal. Still raining. Finally, she was ready to start writing...

I'm lost, dear Alice.

I have no idea what I'm doing here. I just seem to have arrived in this place without thinking through the consequences. It's not too late to go back, but I really, really, really want to go forwards. Where is that? I've just about given up everything I didn't want back in London, but I have no idea what I DO want out here. I feel like a stranger everywhere, like I don't belong anywhere. Nothing fits.

I'm lost. No direction looks like the obvious way to go. I can stay here and just try to be a better person in a cute cottage and a little café in a small town in the middle of nowhere. If you live where nothing happens you can never be tested.

Is this enough? Is this it? Am I just hiding from real life?

The letter stopped there. Bekki didn't sign her name on the bottom. That was the first time that she had done that. The words still sit there in Notebook Number Three looking stark. There was no reply. The page after it was left blank. That night, Bekki sat on the sofa for a very long time listening to the rain dripping from the leaky guttering outside the kitchen window. She didn't finish the hot chocolate and Baileys. After a while she fell asleep.

The next day, Bekki went to work in the café. She was finally starting to get the hang of the till and Alf's acerbic sense of humour. There was always a good phone signal in town. During her morning break, Bekki sent a text message to all the friends she had left in her contact list, plus the same one to her sister. It simply said: *'Feeling a little bit lost today.'* She got lots of encouraging messages back from almost everyone. They sent pithy little sayings like, 'Turn that frown upside down :)' and other succinct messages of support. A couple of people asked 'R U OK?' in the text speak of the time, to which Bekki replied: 'I'm fine. Just a slow day.' Her sister simply sent back 'Love Ya! X' All of this made Bekki smile.

It was the twelfth of January. The Number One single in the UK was *Gotta Get Thru This* by Daniel Bedingfield. Aside from the terrible text-speak spelling, everything in Bekki's world was beginning to collide.

The reason that last letter never did get a reply, not from Alice, or even Rebecca, was that being lost was part of it, as Bekki would realise much later. Not all journeys are full of car games and service station sandwiches. This one was going to take a while and would be as uncomfortable as Swindon to Rhyl in a snow storm, with no toilet breaks or Ginsters pasties.

It had been eighteen months since Bekki had sat in that holiday cottage garden. On that day, when she decided that her whole life needed to escape the deceptions of the world and become truly purposeful, she had honestly thought it would be done by now. But then, personal development isn't as easy as it looks on TV.

Chapter 15

Weeks had turned into months since Bekki had written that last letter. The pages of Notebook Number Three were getting filled up with lists and plans and ideas for things to do with the cottage and its garden in time for Summer. Paint charts and TV makeover shows were an engrossing distraction from the discomfort of self-reflection. That particular mirror had its face turned towards the wall well into April of that year. Alice said nothing. She was always patient. After all, she didn't say anything for the first twenty-eight years.

There had been a couple of visits down to London to see her parents and catch up with some old friends. Every time she went back there, Bekki felt more and more like a stranger in her old city. And every time she came back to Suffolk, she felt more and more like she was at home. She had always felt welcome in the place. Over the months, she discovered that there were many people in the area who had come from Hackney and Tottenham and Walthamstow. It was as if the M11 had been built as a corridor for the sole purpose of getting them all there.

The country lanes and A-roads were familiar to her now, and Bekki enjoyed watching the seasons change outside the kitchen window. Knife crime and graffiti had been replaced with fly tipping and boy racers in souped-up Nissan Micras. It wasn't ideal, but it was a tolerable swap. She imagined it must be what Barnet was like in the nineteen fifties.

It had been a milder than average winter in Europe that year. The snowdrops and daffodils that Bekki had planted in the garden had sprung up two weeks before Mrs Sudley next door had said they would. The old lady blamed the corporate seed and bulb manufacturers for tampering with global genetics and was surprisingly knowledgeable on the subject. Bekki blamed global warming, but Mrs Sudley said she'd physically fight anyone who tried to install wind farms near the village because they played havoc with her pacemaker. She had no scientific basis for this belief. She would, however, welcome fields full of solar panels because it gave the badgers shade in the summer. She was a complex woman.

In the middle of April there was an unseasonable cold snap. Bekki got up one morning to find hard frost all over the garden, quietly freezing her newly planted young lettuces to death. She put on her warmest fleece and frog-face wellies and went outside to check on the little vegetable patch that she'd sown at the bottom of the garden. Everything looked cold and sad. The packing boxes from the house move were still in the shed that had not yet been turned into her perfect writing den. One of the boxes was full of bits of bubble wrap. Bekki fetched some and carried it to the vegetable patch in an attempt to cover the soil and salvage what she could. She popped a few bubbles on the way. Well, you would, wouldn't you?

'I wouldn't bother, dear.' Mrs Sudley's voice called out over the garden fence. She'd been visiting the old, brick outhouse at the end of her garden. Bekki could hear it flushing in the background. Of course, Mrs Sudley had an inside toilet. In fact, she had two. One downstairs in her utility room extension, and one upstairs next to the bidet she kept the toilet brush in. She just liked to avail herself of the outside facilities for movements whose scent might linger longer than any air freshener she was yet to find in a major supermarket, and she'd tried them all. She usually went down to the bottom of the garden after her second cup of tea with malted milks for dunking.

Bekki glanced up and smiled at the old lady. 'What was that?' she said.

'I said, I wouldn't bother, dear,' Mrs Sudley repeated.

'I thought the plastic might protect the plants.'

'Too late for that. Jack Frost has done his work. I blame Monsanto,' she continued. 'Fifty years ago I could plunge my parsnips into a bucket of ice and still have a roast on Sunday.'

'Don't parsnips grow underground?' asked Bekki.

'All the same, it's Big Pharma to blame, you mark my words.'

Bekki thought of correcting the old girl by explaining what 'pharma' was actually short for, but she'd been brought up to respect her elders. 'I think I'll cover them over anyway. It can't do any more damage than they've already had.'

'Whatever,' said Mrs Sudley with a shrug. The choice of language quite surprised Bekki. 'I'm going in now, dearie,' she said. 'It's freezing out here and this housecoat's only nylon.'

The old lady shuffled back indoors humming

something by Tom Jones and closed the door behind her. A silence fell upon the garden. It was that particular kind of silence that happens only when the temperature falls below zero. Even the birds were quiet. Bekki finished tucking in what was left of the small vegetable patch and stood to look around at her garden. Everything was still. There was no breeze. The sky was the palest blue, almost white. Winter had no right to be there in April. It felt like an intruder.

Bekki put a couple of leftover bits of bubble wrap away and bolted the door of the shed. She didn't pop any more bubbles. She was too sad to try. She walked slowly down the stepping stone path and into the cottage, shut the back door behind her and put the kettle on. While she waited for it to boil, she went upstairs to put on her warmest pyjamas and the fluffy boot slippers with the dangling pom-poms that her mother had given her last Christmas. It was Friday. She didn't have another shift at the café for three more days.

She stayed in the same pyjamas for the whole weekend. She didn't even wash her hair. Over the next couple of days, Bekki ate only 'easy' food. Namely, five jacket potatoes with cheese, three packets of biscuits, and a loaf-and-a-half's worth of toast with various spreads and toppings, including peanut butter, Marmite, hazelnut spread, and, in a moment of whimsy, sliced banana and vanilla cake frosting. She also watched eight episodes of *Friends* on DVD, a variety of shows set in a variety of auction houses, and nine hours of a shopping channel that specialised in gems. Bekki was tempted, but she didn't buy anything. She wondered who did. The female presenter selling the

Diamonique bracelets and Pearlique earrings made it sound like everybody was queueing up to grab a bargain before it was too late. 'And I'm just being told there's only two sets of nipple studs left in the blue, so pick up that phone!' Julian would have loved her.

On Monday evening Bekki had another jacket potato. This time she added beans in order to mix it up a little. It was still unseasonably cold outside. She went to the kitchen and switched on the outside light. It lit up the garden with a pale, sterile glow. The bubble wrap was still in place over the vegetable patch. She wondered if anything was still alive under there. She would check again in the morning.

Bekki turned off the outside light and the garden fell dark. The silhouettes of the shed and surrounding trees stood black and cold against the evening sky. It was getting late. She flicked on the TV in order to distract herself from a creeping sadness. It didn't help. It made her even sadder. More than that, it broke her heart.

A couple of hours later, she sat down and wrote a letter. She wrote it very slowly. Deep sadness is never a fast-moving thing.

Dear Alice, Dear Me, Dear Anybody!

Tonight I watched the news on ITV. I didn't mean to. I normally manage to avoid it very successfully because it's not 'news.' It's 'bad news.' That's what they should call it. Would it hurt them to use half the programme for good news? There must be some. Perhaps when somebody did a kind thing for no personal gain, or at least some footage of kittens or puppies, they could show that. Something to bring hope? I think that's why I'm writing this letter. I need some hope from somewhere. Anywhere.

The main news item tonight was about a famine in Sudan, far away from my TV screen but right there in my living room in full colour with surround sound. The world is so connected now. It's instant. One minute you're in Guatemala, the next minute you're wracking your brains to remember the name of that actor because it's worth a million pounds on a quiz show. But tonight, I didn't switch channels when the news came on.

There is a severe drought. No rain in that country for two whole years. Crops have failed and animals are dying in the fields because they have no food or water. People are walking for miles and miles, some carrying children and all the essential things they own, which is not much. Do any of us own many essential things? The people are walking to makeshift charity centres in the hope that they will be fed before they die. One woman stopped to give birth on the way, and now she has another mouth to feed. The charities are running out of food and water too. It's devastating. It's a famine of biblical proportions. The man on the news said that somebody is dying of hunger every forty-eight seconds. As I watched the pictures on TV, nine more people starved to death. I did the maths. They died.

What can I do? I feel so helpless. I sat there in front of the TV and cried. Not big sobs, just hot tears falling silently down my face. Was it pity or shock? Or shame at my own hypocrisy?

This isn't the first famine in the world, and it probably won't be the last. I've seen this kind of thing before. I remember watching Live Aid with mum and dad in the eighties. The gig was amazing, the pictures of starving children were heartbreaking, and I watched it all the way through along with a billion other people. But I didn't feel like this. There wasn't the same sense of helplessness.

What can I do? There's no point in not eating. I can't send my dinner to Africa! It would be rotten by the time it got there. I could stop wasting food. Stop buying big 'bargain' packs of stuff and throwing half of it in the bin. That should be happening anyway. Mrs Sudley never wastes a pie nowadays. So, I throw less in the bin. How does that help them? I could send a donation to one of the charities, but I can't afford much. Even if I sent everything I could afford, that would only feed someone for a few weeks. Even if it lasted a few months, what then?

What can I do? I could go and work for Oxfam or Save the Children, like the people on the news who were describing all this horror to the cameras. But that would mean changing the whole course of my life, and I don't honestly think I can. I'm not sure I could make the sacrifice, because that's what it would be. Does that make me a bad person? In any case, the charity can only do so much. That's why they all look exhausted. They're so brave they put me to shame. Is that what I should be feeling - shame? Live Aid was supposed to change things. Comic Relief, Children In Need, it doesn't seem to have even touched the sides. Why are people still starving? What can I do?

Seriously, what can I do? Is there an answer to this question? I'm asking it but nothing's coming back.

After the news came the usual ad break. There were four ads in that slot. The first was for running shoes. Then a new high performance car. Then an ad for shampoo, because apparently, 'I'm worth it!' Then came a loud and colourful ad featuring buckets and buckets of fried chicken with a secret blend of herbs and spices. That's when I switched off the TV. I couldn't stand it. The comparison was obscene.

I sat in silence for over an hour. It was dark outside and so quiet that I could hear the newsreader's voice still echoing in my head. 'Right now in Africa...' I didn't know what to do. The adverts looked so wrong. Even if they'd been right, they couldn't cleanse my eyes of what I had seen. The pictures had burned into me. I feel helpless and hopeless. How many other people are feeling like this? Did anyone else watch it? Or was there something better on the other channel?

What can I do? What's the point of trying to make my life all nice and clean and true when human beings in their millions are suffering and dying through war and poverty and hunger? What am I doing? What can I do? Does anybody else even care? Did anybody else watch it and feel shame and impotence? Or did they just switch over to the quiz show, like I normally do?

I'm stuck. I need some hope. I need to find out what the point of all this is. I need to know if anything in my life makes a difference in the world, and if it ever can. Please help.

Love,

Bekki, Rebecca... whoever the hell I am!!

Something had clearly shifted in Bekki. Something big and real. There had been previous cries for help in the first two notebooks, notably that very first appeal in the garden of the holiday cottage, but this one was deeper. It came from a different place. It was the sort of cry that comes from young children when they first come across deceit or cruelty. It's a shock to all, but the passing of years and experience becomes a sedative. It dulls the pain.

For the first time, I decided to step in and write back to Bekki, accompanied by Alice. It was meant as an introduction to the whole area that was causing her so much distress. It would not be possible to resolve such a big issue with just one letter. Perhaps not even with one lifetime.

Dear Bekki and Rebecca,

We feel your pain. The more you try to lift the veil on the world's deception, the more you will feel it too. That cannot be helped. You are beginning to remove the anaesthetic that causes such numbness and ignorance in our societies. Some of this is wilful, but some is innocent, and much is understandable. For, who would willingly wish to feel the pain that exists in the human race? If you were to try and feel it all at once, it would certainly crush you.

167

Understand this: If you decide to undertake a search for truth in life, you'd better be prepared to find it. All of it, not just the bits that you personally like. Not just the bits that are pleasant to you.

Small steps are the way to go, so that you don't become overwhelmed by the magnitude of it all. Accept the fact that you don't know everything, and nor does anybody else. Above all, be kind. First to yourself, and then to others.

You told us a story that happened in a supermarket car park. What there is to learn from this story is a universal principle. It's how viruses work. They multiply when they find a host. If you're kind to one person, and they are kind to one more, then you have changed three lives, not just one. And on it goes.

Hope lies in understanding and acceptance. It's also good not to throw food away, always!

You ask, 'does anybody else care?' but what makes you so different? You are also 'anybody.' Others ask this question at difficult times, just like you. You are not alone. Many people feel the pain. Recognise them and share the burden together wherever you can. The weight feels heavier if you believe that you're carrying it on your own.

With love and care,

Rea and Alice.

PS: None of this journey is compulsory. Never forget that. You can step off this path that you've chosen and go back to the life you were living any time you like. Nobody would blame you. There is always choice.

PPS: You don't feel the same as you did when you watched Live Aid because you're not the same person anymore. Nobody is.

Bekki went back to Notebook Number Three and read this letter many times over the years. She took the 'PS' very seriously and thought about going back to London and her old life on more than one occasion. But she knew that she couldn't. Just like the news item about the famine, some things once seen cannot be unseen. Likewise, some things once thought cannot easily be forgotten.

There was a brief response to this letter from Bekki, written underneath it at the time. She simply wrote:

'Who's Rea?'

Alice replied in her best handwriting.

'Rea is you in the future and the present all at once.'

Underneath that, Bekki simply drew a smiley face and coloured it in with a yellow felt tip pen a couple of days later when she felt better.

The next day was a Tuesday and Bekki had a morning shift in the café. The pictures from last night's news story were still fresh in her mind. So was her letter and its response. The first half hour of her working day was spent cleaning down the kitchen in preparation for an upcoming surprise visit from the local Health Inspector.

Bekki did ask how anyone could possibly know that a surprise visit was about to happen. Didn't that defeat the object? Alf replied with his now familiar tap on the nose with accompanying wink. Ruby simply said, 'It's not *what* you know, love,' expecting Bekki to complete the second half of that sentence for herself, which she did, of course.

Whatever the local health authority employees could possibly be gaining in backhanders from a small café in Stowmarket was anybody's guess. Or was it that Alf knew where all the bodies were buried? Bekki simply accepted it and was relieved that she could spend some time out the back with some bleach, a heavy pan scourer, and her thoughts.

By eleven o'clock, the morning rush had subsided. Ruby made three frothy coffees and invited Bekki to come and sit with her and Alf for a break at the best table by the big window. Alf broke his customary three sachets of white sugar over his mug and pushed the wooden sugar bowl towards Bekki. She took a brown one and thanked him.

Ruby's eyes were searching Bekki's face as she stirred her coffee and blew across the top to cool it. 'You alright, love?' she asked. 'You're very quiet today.'

Bekki's mouth formed a smile that didn't quite reach up to her eyes. 'Yes, I'm fine, thanks.'

'No, you're not,' corrected Alf. 'People always say that the first time you ask them when they're not fine at all. Why do they do that when they're obviously not fine? Is it just so that we have to ask them again? It just wastes bloody time. Attention seeking, is it?'

'No, I...' Bekki couldn't complete the thought.

'Stop it, Alf,' interjected Ruby.

'True though, isn't it?' he insisted. 'We Brits are all a bunch of hypocrites. You don't get this in Crete.'

'When were you ever in Crete?' questioned Ruby with a smirk.

'During the war.'

'What war?'

'I'm not allowed to tell you. I swore a pledge.'

Ruby rolled her eyes. 'Stupid old man.' She turned back to Bekki and tried again. 'Seriously, what's wrong, love? You don't seem yourself.'

'It's nothing.'

'Yes, it is,' insisted Alf. 'Stop saying that it isn't.'

'Okay, okay. It's just that I feel a bit down today, that's all. Can we not talk about it?' said Bekki.

'See?' Alf slapped his thigh, took a sip of his coffee, and then proceeded to pour two more sachets of white sugar into his mug while whistling the theme to *Born Free* for no reason at all. The women watched him patiently. They'd seen it all before. Then, satisfied with himself, Alf stopped whistling and changed his tone. He leaned forward a little in his chair and tilted his head to one side. This caused him to look more softly into Bekki's eyes. 'Something happened last night, didn't it, girl?'

Bekki nodded. 'I'm fine. I'm just being a bit stupid, really.'

'We won't laugh,' assured Ruby, 'will we, Alf?'

'I'm promising nothing,' he said.

Ruby gave Alf a gentle slap around the back of the head and moved the sugar bowl out of his reach. 'If someone's upset you, you can tell us about it and we'll help if we can. Unless it's Alf that upset you. I can't sack him because I don't pay him, do I? I can always stop feeding him, though.'

'You can try.' Alf humphed, 'but I've got the card for the Cash and Carry. You'll change your tune when we run out of chips.'

'That was it,' said Bekki. 'It's about food. Or rather the lack of it.' She started voicing her thoughts and couldn't stop until they were all out of her head. She told Ruby and Alf about the images she'd seen on the news; about the famine that was going on while cafés and restaurants and supermarkets all over the world were throwing good food in the bin; about her frustration at being able to do nothing to make it better; about feeling like a hypocrite as she piled chips on people's plates and selected the biggest cake at the bakery counter every time she went to Sainsbury's. And she spoke on and on as Ruby and Alf sipped their coffees and listened until she stopped.

When Bekki did stop, it was sudden. It surprised her and she felt her cheeks flush. She must have sounded like a sentimental idiot. *'What a naïve little child I am,'* she thought, *'that's what they must think.'* But she was wrong, they didn't think that at all.

Alf spoke first. 'Is that it?' he said.

Ruby slapped him round the back of the head again, this time a bit harder. 'Don't take any notice of him,' she said. 'I watched that news report last night.'

'So did I, you silly woman. I watched it with you. Don't you remember? Or have you been skipping your HRT again?'

'Of course I remember. You ate all my chocolate Hob Nobs, you greedy old git.'

As this little domestic drama played out at the table, Bekki felt increasingly awkward. 'Sorry,' she said, 'I shouldn't have mentioned it. I'm fine, honest. It's not like people haven't starved before. There's nothing I can do about it anyway.'

Alf folded his arms across his chest, staring hard into Bekki's face, then swung back precariously on his chair. Just as he was about to tip backwards onto the hard floor, Ruby pushed down on the wooden seat between his knees and he rocked back into position without batting an eyelid. 'Do you think you're the only person who feels these things?' said Alf.

'No, but…'

'Listen, girl, that kind of thing has been going on for ever, just like human greed and cruelty.'

'And human care and empathy,' added Ruby.

'Yes, but…' Bekki interjected again, but she didn't really know what she was going to say. Luckily, Alf wasn't giving her a chance.

'There are two types of people in this world. Those who care and try to make a difference, and those who don't give a shit and do nothing.'

'No, Alf,' interrupted Ruby. 'There are three. There are also those who care but don't know what to do about it.'

Alf thought about this, then nodded his agreement. 'Fair enough. I stand corrected.'

'So, my dear girl…' Ruby turned to Bekki. 'Which one do you want to be?'

There was a pause around the table. The older folk

waited and sipped their coffees. Bekki answered the question softly. 'I want to do something, but I don't know what that is.'

'So, you're type number three,' said Ruby. 'Now we're getting somewhere. The next step is to move you towards type number one, because caring and doing nothing can only go on for so long. Eventually you make a choice, whether you like it or not. You either stop caring or start doing something about it. It's the only way to save your sanity.'

The café was completely devoid of customers for the rest of Bekki's shift. It was as if the town knew that it had to give the three people inside some time to talk without interruption. As if Alf had turned the 'Open' sign around to 'Closed' so they could talk in peace. Bekki checked the door on her way out later. The sign was hanging in its usual place. Two young mums with toddlers in pushchairs came in through the door as she opened it to leave, chatting loudly together about the doings of some absent third mum as they entered. Bekki held the door open for them and turned to wave goodbye to Ruby and Alf. Ruby was already busy greeting the mums. Alf had disappeared out the back of the café. Probably going for his fourth cigarette break of the day. The sign on the café door had said 'Open' the whole time.

Bekki went straight home. She didn't put the TV on at all that night. Instead, she dug out a cardboard box full of CDs that was still taped shut under the bed and dusted off the old battery-operated CD/Radio player that she kept for emergencies and power cuts. She ripped open the box, closed her eyes and dipped her hand in to pick out a disc at random. Fate would decide her soundtrack. What came out in her hand was an album by R.E.M., which happened to be one of her favourites. It was just the right mix of seriousness and inspiration. She put it on and sat down to write a letter.

Dear Alice and Rea,

You were both right. Of course you were. I'm not alone. None of us are 'the only ones.' We can only know that when we start to look at others without judging too quickly. We only find out when we speak out, not only saying how we feel but asking how someone else feels. And then, sometimes the most surprising people say: 'You too, huh?' How arrogant I was to think it was just me.

I had a good chat with Ruby and Alf at the café today. Every Friday night, they make a big pot of soup and sandwiches and set up a table round the back of the supermarket. I didn't think there would be any homeless people in a small, Suffolk town like this. They're hidden away somewhere during the day, but Ruby says they feed about a dozen people on an average night. 'Not all of them are homeless, but all of them are hungry,' she said. I had no idea they did something like this. It had never occurred to me to ask. I'm going to help them next Friday.

I can't sort out all the problems of the world. I can't even solve one famine in one African country. But, like Ruby said, we can all do something, no matter how small. So, to not do that something is a disservice to the world and to yourself. When you show care, you give others permission to join in, and that can only be a good thing. Look at me - I've joined in with them as soon as I found out that they were doing something to make the world a little better. Even if we can't be instigators, we can certainly be collaborators.

It does feel like a small thing, but it's a start, isn't it? I've begun. I want to be someone who cares and tries to find a way to do something about it. I don't want to be crushed by the weight of the world's problems. And that's where you were right. It already feels lighter because I know of two other people who care. And this is just one café in one little town. There must be many more people. I'm going to keep looking out for them.

With hope,
Bekki x

The response to this letter was very short. It came from Rea alone.

Dear Bekki,
Keep going.
Rea.

That cold snap in April was brief. It only lasted two more days. By the end of the week, Bekki had taken the bubble wrap off the vegetable patch and discovered, to her surprise and delight, that almost all of the fledgling vegetables were still alive. Mrs Sudley was equally impressed and asked if it were possible to buy bubble wrap on the interweb. Bekki offered to save her the trouble and gave her some of the spare sheets from the shed. She received a family-sized, homemade apple and rhubarb pie in return. Not just Mr Sudley's half like normal, but one baked specially for the occasion. Bekki took it with her when she went to help Ruby and Alf the next Friday night. Every slice was eaten.

Bekki continued working her shifts in the café and helping out on Friday nights round the back of the supermarket. As the nights got milder and the days got longer, more people would come from further afield to seek out Ruby and Alf. There was always enough soup and sandwiches to feed everybody who turned up. Ruby made sure of that. After Bekki told Mrs Sudley about the Stowmarket Soup Kitchen, there were regular apple and rhubarb pies from her too. The old lady had no idea that there were homeless people in her local town, but she was very good at spreading the news about it. Pretty soon, other ladies at Mrs Sudley's knit and natter group were baking pies and cakes and leaving them at the café for Ruby to share with whoever might need them. It all helped.

There was one last letter at the end of Notebook Number Three. It was really a letter to Bekki herself rather than to anybody else. It was the first time that she had addressed one of her letters in this way:

Dear Me,

I could really hear the birds singing this morning.
No, I don't think I know how to emphasise it properly in writing...I could REALLY hear the birds singing this morning. What I mean is that it wasn't

just random sound or something, it was as if I could understand what they were saying. In London, it was just background noise. I hardly heard the chirping above the traffic and the people. I guess I thought it would be the same out here.

It's springtime now. The birds sing louder in the spring than they do in the autumn and their songs are more repetitive. The important thing is that I noticed that! I didn't know I could, now I can't stop hearing the little critters.

This might sound like garbage because I can't explain it properly, but I know exactly what I mean. Honestly. I've only written this down so that I can remember it in the future. That's all. This is a happy note.

Big hugs,
Me x

And that was the end of Notebook Number Three.

Chapter 16

Notebook Number Four turned out to be quite different in its content to the first three notebooks. The main departure was that there were a lot of attempts within it to write what could be called essays or articles - some might call them opinion pieces - rather than Bekki's more heartfelt letters or simpler scribbled notes and lists. This came out of a growing sense of confidence that Bekki had for getting down her thoughts on paper. That, and a misplaced sense that she should be taking everything much more seriously and writing 'properly' for posterity. This wasn't really her style and so it didn't last long.

Fewer letters to Alice or Rea are written in Notebook Number Four. This was because Ruby and Alf were getting to know Bekki and could tell when something was troubling her. The questions still came, just as big and difficult, but Ruby had a way of sitting Bekki down with them and bringing her back to earth at the same time.

There are more pages crossed out in the first half of Notebook Number Four than pages that are not crossed out. In fact, the second half of it remains blank to this day, abandoned in favour of starting afresh with Notebook Number Five. There is evidence that many pages were neatly torn out too. Whatever was once written on them has long been forgotten. Not everything has to be preserved for the future. Some things are very definitely best put in the bin. Just ask almost any dead author whose widow/mother/agent finds a discarded manuscript in a sock drawer with a shopping list scribbled on the back, only to publish it posthumously in hardback and have it panned by online reviewers. Or even worse, have it hailed universally as an undiscovered masterpiece when the author is long gone and not able to enjoy the plaudits or the book royalties.

But back to Notebook Number Four.

To provide a flavour for the reader, here is a perfect example of one of those serious attempts at an essay by Bekki. It was written out very carefully with a fountain pen that she had bought at the Stowmarket Stationery Nook next door to the café. It was important to have the right writing implement for these essays in order to add some perceived extra importance. Thankfully, this is a very brief specimen of one of those missives.

ON POLITICS by Rebecca Reeves

I've given it a lot of thought, and I've come to the conclusion that politics is a big waste of time and money. They waste far too much time arguing about whose party is better at fooling most of the people most of the time instead of fixing the roads and building hospitals, and they waste far too much money on PR companies and bribes. The only way to stop politicians arguing and get them to actually work for the people they're paid to serve is to remove any kind of competition. In other words, ensure that all political parties govern together without trying to get one over on each other all the time. If they can't do that, remove politicians altogether and replace them with service companies that can actually fix things and keep them working on time. If that doesn't work, we'll have to have a revolution.

Also, politics just divides people and makes them angry.

To be fair to Bekki, she had come up with as good a solution as any other that had been put forward by any number of academics from the major universities of the world. And a couple of those had even been given Nobel Prizes for Economics.

Politics was a worldwide issue that was far too big and ugly for Bekki to tackle at this stage in her development journey. If and when she was to achieve a higher state of human evolution, she probably wouldn't bother with politics at all. There would be far more important things to fill her time.

Even more remarkably, and with an inflated sense of confidence that seems extraordinary now, Bekki had a go at writing an insightful essay on an even bigger topic.

ON RELIGION by Rebecca Reeves
After much soul searching on the subject, I've come to the conclusion that all religions say the same thing at their core: be kind to each other and everything will turn out fine. I don't know why anybody has such a problem with that. I also don't know why all the religions need so many books and churches and

temples and priests. They could say it all on a t-shirt and save a lot of money, not to mention all the wars. And speaking of money, too many organised religions are too keen to separate their congregations from it by rattling collection boxes.

On reflection, I may have oversimplified this subject. It is quite big. I will give it more thought and then come back to it later.

Bekki never did come back and write a further essay on religion. In many ways, she didn't have to. Sometimes the most profound things are hard to swallow because they seem too simple, particularly at such a convoluted age as the beginning of the twenty-first century, when completing a tax return was more difficult than growing a carrot in a sports bag full of socks. In general, people expect wisdom to be complicated. That comes down to formal education. It also comes down to comparing wisdom to opinion and truth to preference.

Bekki never wrote another essay on politics either, which is a blessing indeed. Some weeks later, on a shopping trip to the Suffolk metropolis that is Ipswich, she bought herself Notebook Number Five. It sat on her bedside table, pristine and prepared, waiting for something to happen that was worth being recorded.

Chapter 17

Exactly three years to the day that Bekki had her epiphany in the garden of that holiday cottage, the doorbell rang. She always remembered the date on purpose. It was circled on every wall calendar and in every diary that she had ever owned since that first visit to Suffolk. The calendar that happened to be gracing the kitchen wall on the fourteenth of July two-thousand-and-three, was called *Great British Bangers*. This could have been a suitable title for the kind of date marker that graces the walls of many a garage and MOT centre across the land, but it wasn't that kind of calendar. It was actually a freebie from the pork butcher that supplied *Tiffin Teas* with their breakfast meats. The month of July featured a rather overstuffed, over-sauced Suffolk Gold with a side of Colman's mustard. This calendar and its vibrant colour images would be responsible for convincing Bekki to become a vegetarian by the end of that year.

It was Monday morning, not quite eleven o'clock, and Bekki was still in her pyjamas. She wasn't on the rota at the café that day, otherwise she would definitely not still be in her pyjamas. She did, however, have a recurring dream for several years where she turned up for work in that very same nightwear only to discover, to her horror, that her pockets were full of chips seasoned with vinegar.

She always woke up before the vinegar seepage spread to her thighs.

She opened the door expecting it to be Fiona the post lady, who she had taken to having an in-joke with every morning:

'Have you got a letter for me today?' Bekki would call out.

'Sure. How about an 'E'?'

'Ha, ha, ha!'

'Ho, ho, ho!'

But it wasn't the post lady who rang the doorbell that morning. It was Jake. He had no idea that the date was significant. That made his visit on the fourteenth of July two-thousand-and-three even more remarkable.

The last person Bekki expected to see on the doorstep was Jake. She would have been less shocked if it had been her mother wearing a Grateful Dead t-shirt and smoking a spliff saying, 'Hey, man! Have you got any cake?' Jake hadn't phoned or written or even texted for three years. Bekki was so surprised that she couldn't speak for what felt like a very long ten seconds. This was completely out of character for her.

'Hey, Bekks. It's me!' said Jake with a broad grin.

'Wha...' sort of said Bekki. She knew perfectly well who it was. It didn't stop him checking to make sure.

'It's Jake. Don't you remember?' and he threw out an even broader grin and put up his hands in a surrender pose, in case it helped to jog her memory.

'Wow!' Bekki very nearly swore at this point. The occasion certainly warranted a strong expletive to denote that level of surprise.

'Yeah,' said Jake. 'It's been a while, hasn't it? Nice looking place. Bit different to Finchley Road, eh?'

'Oh, Jake. I'm so sorry.' Bekki managed to compose herself a little and remembered that she was standing in her doorway in her pyjamas. These were quite unique, as pyjamas go. The knee-length, cotton shorts were printed with well-loved images of Winnie the Pooh and Piglet, as originally drawn by popular children's artist, E.H. Shepard. The top - long since separated from its own bottoms - was a V-neck, cap-sleeved t-shirt of faux-satin polyester, emblazoned with the legend 'Check My Booty Out' in sparkly letters. It's unlikely that Pooh and Piglet would have approved of the statement inscribed above them across Bekki's bosom, but we'll never know. E.H. Shepard died in nineteen-seventy-six.

Fiona, the post lady walked by on the other side of the road as Bekki and Jake stood on the doorstep in all kinds of awkwardness. She waved, waiting to be asked for the day's letter. Bekki just waved back, much to Fiona's disappointment, causing her to accidentally deliver the latest copy of *Nuts* magazine through old Mr Lupin's letterbox across the road. That would spice up his cornflakes for sure.

'What am I thinking? Come in, come in,' Bekki said to Jake, and stepped back inside the house to make space for him to enter. Then she remembered what she was wearing, grabbed a long, grey cardigan from one of the hooks behind the front door, and slipped it on over the offending pyjamas. 'I'll put the kettle on and make us a coffee,' said Bekki.

'Great,' said Jake, 'I'm really thirsty.' He wasn't, actually.

But he was a little nervous. It had been three long years, and much had happened to both of them.

Coffee making procedures provided some welcome minutes for Jake to settle himself down, and for Bekki to compose herself. She'd motioned for Jake to sit at the end of the sofa in the living room that faced the window onto the garden. That way, she could prepare refreshments without being observed from where he sat.

She thought about changing out of her pyjamas into day clothes, maybe running a comb through her hair, maybe even brushing her teeth. But that might look like Bekki was embarrassed about her appearance in front of her ex-boyfriend who, quite frankly, looked better than she remembered. Of course, she *was* embarrassed. Jake hadn't even noticed. He was the kind of man who reliably failed to notice if someone had had a haircut, or lost twelve pounds in weight, or replaced their arms with propellers for better aerodynamics. These sorts of things just weren't important to him. They were all on the outside, and he was one of those guys who was genuinely more impressed by what was on the inside of a person. Many claim it. Few actually mean it.

'Do you still take milk and one sugar?' called out Bekki from behind the kitchen door.

'In tea or coffee?' replied Jake.

This caused some respite from awkwardness and made Bekki smile to herself. Jake always answered the question with the same answer. Even if he'd watched the beverage being prepared in front of his face. 'I'm making coffee,' she recapped.

'Oh, yeah,' said Jake.

'So, do you still take milk and one sugar?'

'In tea or coffee?'

'Umm…coffee,' said Bekki.

'Yes, please,' said Jake.

'And in tea?'

'Just coffee, thanks.'

Three years ago, this exchange would have left Bekki frustrated at best, and infuriated at worst. When they first started seeing each other, she had found it endearing. Now, on the fourteenth of July, two-thousand-and-three, she found it sweet again. It caused a tingle of nostalgia that took her by surprise. She stirred the sugar into Jake's coffee and carried a mug for each of them into the living room. Bekki was really hot in her grey cardigan, and not in a good way. She tried her best to look cool as she sat down in the armchair next to the sofa. Her attempt at glacial grace didn't register with Jake at all. He was just really pleased to see her, and very happy that she hadn't slammed the door in his face. He took a sip of his coffee and smiled at Bekki. She smiled back.

'How did you find my address?' she asked.

'Your sister gave it to me.'

'Really?' An unexpected pang of jealousy shot up from her stomach and stuck in her throat. She gave a little cough to loosen it. 'When did you see my sister?'

'She came to one of our gigs in London.'

'Gigs?' Bekki gave a second little cough. This time it was involuntary and a little spit of coffee came out. She wiped her lips with the sleeve of her cardigan as if she meant it. She was getting even hotter. 'Are you in a band now or something?' She half-laughed this question out of her mouth. She wasn't expecting the answer that came.

'Yeah. Didn't Jane tell you?'

'No, she didn't mention it. I only spoke to her last week. She didn't say anything about you at all.'

'Oh, I thought she would have told you,' said Jake quite reasonably.

Bekki sat up a bit straighter in the armchair. It was time to kick her brain into gear. It had been lagging behind the rest of her ever since the doorbell had rung. Perhaps being more upright would help shove some energy up her spine towards her head. The caffeine certainly hadn't kicked in yet and the whole situation seemed like a dream. She needed to focus. 'I thought Jane would have told me too. It's the sort of the thing she loves to share. So,' she continued, attempting nonchalance quite unsuccessfully, 'when did you become a musician then?'

'Well, I'm not really a musician, I'm a bass player,' explained Jake. 'I can't read music or anything, but it turns out you don't need to. I've always had a sense of rhythm, though, so that helps.'

'Wow! That's unbelievable. Bit of a dramatic change of lifestyle for you, isn't it?'

'Yeah,' agreed Jake. 'I do miss Argos sometimes. We used to have a laugh in the warehouse. I'm still in touch with some of them.'

Bekki was both impressed and baffled. 'You mean you're doing music full time?'

'I suppose you could say that, although you get lots of time off. But I am earning money from it, and I'm not doing any other job so, yeah. I guess it's full time.'

'What's the name of your band?'

'Breadroll Caravan.'

A third cough exploded out of Bekki so hard that it forced some coffee out of her nose with great velocity. It landed right in the middle of Jake's mug with a splash. This spectacular feat of accuracy deserved some recognition. Perhaps a standing ovation, or at least a round of applause. It got neither. Jake simply placed his mug gently on the coffee table and brushed a few splashes from his sleeve with his fingers. 'Sorry,' said Bekki. 'I'll make you a fresh one.' But she didn't move from the armchair. She just stared at Jake with renewed interest, not quite knowing what the cool thing to do might be.

Sometimes when people are nervous, or haven't seen ex-partners for a while, they make statements and ask questions that are quite unnecessary just in order to fill empty spaces with words. 'Have you heard of us, then?' asked Jake, to prove this point.

'Have I?' asked Bekki. It was rhetorical. 'Yes, I've heard of you. Jeez! You're famous.'

Jake shrugged. 'Not really,' he said. 'I suppose our singer is, but then that's probably because he went out with…well, I'm not actually allowed to talk about it. I signed a non-disclosure agreement.'

Bekki sprang out of her armchair and onto the sofa next to Jake in one gazelle-like movement. 'You mean the rumours are true?'

'I've said too much.' Jake had never been one to gossip and Bekki's pleas for inside information fell on deaf ears. 'Anyway, we're on MySpace, if you want to check us out.'

'MySpace? What's that?'

'It's a really cool website. There's all kinds of photos

and videos and stuff on there. Are you on the internet here?'

'Yes, but the connection's a bit slow. I'll have a look later, if I've got time.' Bekki tried her best to look unimpressed, but she was gagging to switch on her PC and fire up the dial-up connection.

Jake noticed nothing. 'Any chance of that fresh coffee?' he said. 'Some of mine's been down your nose.'

'Of course. Sorry.' Bekki put the kettle on, hunted for then found the cafetière at the back of the kitchen cupboard that she hardly ever used, and made a 'proper' coffee for them to share. It felt right to serve something better than instant granules. There were a few chocolate biscuits in the bread bin that were still edible too. She put them out on a little plate and brought the whole lot through to the living room on a tray.

The pair sipped coffee, chatted, and sometimes laughed for over an hour. In that time, Bekki even forgot about the pyjamas she was wearing and took off her cardigan. She felt comfortable enough to do so. In fact, she'd forgotten just how comfortable she had always felt in Jake's company. The sun was streaming in through the living room window, lighting up the inglenook and sparkling off the brass coal bucket. Everything was pleasant.

The number one single in the UK on the fourteenth of July two-thousand-and-three was *Crazy in Love* by Beyoncé featuring Jay-Z. It was number one for three weeks. As before, this was merely incidental, but Bekki did begin to wonder whether she had been a bit rash when she dumped Jake.

It turned out that Breadroll Caravan were in the middle

of a UK tour and were due to play in Ipswich that night. By one of many strange coincidences that seemed to follow Bekki around, the band's drummer, Eric, had grown up in Stowmarket. Not only did he know exactly where Bekki's cottage was, he also happened to be the grandson of Mrs Sudley next door. He could also have rewired that dodgy light fitting on Bekki's landing that made the bulb blow every three weeks. He was an electrician before he joined the band. As Jake and Bekki reminisced about old times, Eric, the road crew, and the rest of the band were currently next door eating rhubarb and banana brownies and drinking tea with Bekki's neighbour. It was a small world.

Jake promised to put Bekki on the guest list for the Ipswich gig, and she promised to be there. As they said their farewells at the front door, Bekki reached out her arms for a hug. It was the natural thing to do. Jake obliged and she felt a small kiss on the side of her neck. It was confirmed. She had missed him. The kiss was nice.

Bekki closed the front door and Jake walked to Mrs Sudley's cottage. She ran upstairs to peek around the curtain of the spare bedroom to watch for Jake and his bandmates to leave. It was another ten minutes or so until they did, all piling into a sleek, black minibus. *That singer is much shorter than he looks in the gossip mags,* thought Bekki. Then she went to fetch Notebook Number Five from the bedside table. It was time to write the first entry in the new notebook.

Dear Alice,
*   A new notebook on a new day, and a brand-new revelation.*

Jake came round, right out of the blue, and it was a total shock to see him standing on the doorstep. I only realised afterwards just why it was such a shock. I wasn't expecting a visit and was therefore unprepared for it, but that wasn't it. It was because he wasn't the old Jake that I remembered.

Sure, there were lots of things that were recognisable, and quirks remained, but he was different because time had passed. I last saw him three years ago, and expected him to be exactly the same man with the same history, as if he'd been sat on his sofa killing zombies the whole time without doing anything else. But the years when I didn't see him or know him are now history too... if that makes sense?

When I think about how much has changed in my life over the same time - which is pretty much everything! - how ridiculous that I should think that everybody else has just been standing still. How egocentric am I?!

This has caused me to see how easy it is to fix our view of another person according to the last point we interacted with them. We freeze that person in time in our minds. This means that we become out of date about other people and other places too. I've changed, so why wouldn't they? It's logical. Might be for the better or it might not, but they've got older and had experiences and lived and have new stories to tell.

It seems so obvious as I read this over. Maybe it's not, I don't know. I wonder what Jake saw when

he looked at me today? Did he think I've changed?
I'm going to try very hard not to think of people as
fixed in the past, just as they were the last time I saw
them. Maybe I should start with my parents... or
maybe something a bit easier!
  Bekki xx

Alice's reply came almost immediately.

Dear Bekki,
  You're learning.
  Alice x

PS: You're not particularly egocentric, you're
normal. However, it's no bad thing to be 'different.'

PPS: Isn't it great to start a fresh page in a new
notebook? That's all you have to do with other
people. Start a fresh page each time.

At nine-thirty that evening, Jake stepped on stage at
the Bald Flamingo in Ipswich with his bass guitar and his
bandmates. The venue erupted. Bekki was sitting in the
middle of the balcony with Pinko, Breadroll Caravan's
German sound engineer, taking full advantage of her
Access All Areas laminated pass. Unlike most of the road
crew, the origin of Pinko's nickname was a mystery. He
had neither pink hair nor even one item of rose-coloured
clothing, his politics were never discussed, to anybody's
recollection, and he preferred his drinks golden yellow
and lager-flavoured. As the noise of the audience's whoops

and cheers ascended to the rafters, Pinko nudged up the master volume and nodded to himself with satisfaction as the opening chord of the first song rang out. He turned to Bekki and smiled through a nod. She smiled back like she knew exactly what all those buttons and faders were for. She didn't.

Bekki found herself sitting on that darkened balcony in a state of confusion. She was half bloated around the ego, thanks to the backstage pass swinging on its lanyard around her neck, and half astonished that she was actually watching her ex-boyfriend Jake playing an actual instrument in a proper music venue full of live humans. Not zombies or aliens on a screen, but actual live human beings. Not only that, but the large audience appeared to know all the songs and insisted on singing along to every chorus while flailing their arms and jumping around in what can only loosely be described as 'dancing.'

As the set progressed, and the sweat to sweet-smell ratio in the venue tipped towards the former, Bekki relaxed a little in her privileged place. She leaned forwards in her seat, resting her forearms on the balcony ledge, and gazed at the young people who were getting sticky below and loving it. *They must be crazy*, she thought. *It's baking in here.* The realisation then hit her, with even more discomfort than the perspiration pricking her underarms, that she felt old.

It was two-thousand-and-three. Bekki was thirty-one years old. To those over fifty, the word 'only' would be placed before Bekki's age here, followed by a slight eye roll or a 'tut.' To those under eighteen, Bekki was almost as old as their parents. In some Southern states of America, she was almost old enough to be one of their grandparents. It was all relative, and Bekki knew that, but at that precise moment in time she felt old nevertheless.

How did knowledge of Breadroll Caravan's line up pass her by? They were clearly well established. She'd read about the singer and his alleged love life and the guitarist's drug bust. Perhaps the press had never mentioned the bassist and drummer. Who does? But the band's fame had even reached the cultural outpost of Ipswich, judging by the speed at which the tour t-shirts were flying out of the merchandise stall downstairs.

It had been years since Bekki had listened to popular radio, or any kind or radio, come to think of it. Since moving out of the city, she had completely stopped buying CDs, which were the popular music medium of the day, and hardly ever fished out her old ones to play at home. It dawned on Bekki then that she couldn't remember consciously deciding to eliminate music from her life, but it seemed like she had. Suddenly she missed it.

What else had she eliminated? In her search for a cleaner kind of life, she had excluded everything that might have been responsible for the deception or hypocrisy that filled the world and made her unhappy, but she had been brutal. It was time to look again and reintroduce some babies that had been thrown out with the bath water. She used to love music. Not all of it, obviously, but there was much that made her want to dance, to sing, brought joy, moved her to tears, and it always helped while doing the ironing. She vowed to go through her CD collection when she got home. It had to be cleaner than watching TV.

Before Breadroll Caravan had finished their second

encore, Bekki slipped out the back door of the Bald Flamingo. Before she left, she thanked Pinko for letting her sit next to the sound desk and asked him to say goodbye to Jake. Tomorrow the band would be gigging at King Tut's Wah Wah Hut in Glasgow, thanks to some wildly inept itinerary planning by the band's agent. Four more weeks of zig-zagging across the UK was to be followed by a tour of Eastern Europe, and then Japan.

Bekki left her phone number with Pinko to pass on to Jake. It would be several months before she saw him again. In the meantime, there was always MySpace.

Chapter 18

Social media is a term that pretty much everyone on the planet is now familiar with. People at the farthest flung corners of the Earth continue to sign up and fill the endless scrolling pages of these twenty-first century megaliths. It's not uncommon to see pictures of what someone had for breakfast in Burundi, or updates on the cuteness of cats in Crete. But back in the year two-thousand-and-three, when Jake knocked on the door of Bluebell Cottage, the phrase hadn't yet been invented. Much has happened in the last twenty years via the internet. People born in the nineteen sixties and seventies, however, are still waiting for the hover boards they were promised by the popular TV science show, *Tomorrow's World*. They also promised greater leisure time in the digital age. Everybody's still waiting.

After watching Breadroll Caravan's minibus drive out of view, Bekki had rushed to the spare bedroom to switch on her PC. The familiar screeches and squawks of the internet dial-up connection filled the room. Bekki covered her ears until the cacophony subsided and she was finally connected to the World Wide Web, much to her relief. *There must be a better way of doing this*, she thought. Don't worry, Wi-Fi is coming, Bekki.

A quick search around the internet and the wonder

that was MySpace appeared on her monitor screen. Bekki had done a bit of work on PCs at Pitch Perfect, so she found her way around the site without too much difficulty. She typed 'Breadroll Caravan' into the search box and then waited as a new image scrolled, chunk by chunk, from the top of the screen to the bottom.

Young people of today: opening a new page or image in the olden days of the early noughties took around ten to fifteen seconds, if you were lucky and your mum wasn't using the landline in the kitchen to call the speaking clock. Can you imagine? A hardened influencer these days could create three TikTok reels in that time.

The picture on the PC's monitor finally unrolled itself in its entirety, and there they were in all their glory, one of the coolest Brit Pop bands of the day - and Bekki knew one of them intimately! She was impressed. She read through the biog and clicked around the photos and discography on the MySpace page, lingering on some of the live shots of Jake with his bass guitar. It was hard to believe that this was the same guy that she had dumped back in London, but there was his wavy hairline for all to see. No-one else had a hairline like that.

Bekki saved the page to her Favourites. She would open it and look at the pictures regularly. She wondered about creating her own page. It was free and relatively simple to anyone under forty. But what would she say to the world? MySpace was full of bands and artists and authors and people with interesting jobs in the media. Who would want to read about her? No, this wasn't the site for her. A blog would be a much better fit, but they hadn't quite taken off at the time.

A couple of years later, Jane called Bekki on her mobile for a catch up. Moving away from London meant the sisters hardly saw each other. Jane was a stranger to the Greater Anglia Rail Network and she had still not passed her driving test, which was something her mother regularly mentioned but that Jane cared very little about. She had a way of finding free lifts whenever she needed them. The distance had prompted regular calls, though, and this was evidence that Jane missed seeing her big sister, even though she wouldn't admit it. This was all about to change. Virtually, at least.

Bekki's mobile phone rang and her sister's name and number popped on to the screen. 'Hi Jane,' said Bekki.

'Yo, sis!' said Jane, barely audible amidst a wall of sound.

'I can hardly hear you,' yelled Bekki into the phone. 'Where are you?'

'What?' yelled back Jane just as loud. 'I can't hear you.'

'I said, where are you? It's really noisy.'

'Hang on a minute, it's really noisy. I'll go outside.' Loud echoes of conversation and laughter and clinking glasses gave way to acceptable levels of background traffic noise. 'Can you hear me now?' asked Jane.

'Yes, that's better. Where are you?'

'I'm outside the Crane & Marmoset. They've got a new seating area by the bottle banks.'

A sudden clatter and smash of glass caused Bekki to wince and pull the phone away from her ear. 'Bloody hell! That was loud.'

'Sorry, sis. They've gone back in now. How are you doing?'

'I'm good. What about you?'

'I'm brilliant. I've just got on this thing called *Facebook*. Have you heard of it?'

'No, what is it? Some kind of moisturiser?'

'Ha! Silly arse. No, it's a social network. You've got to get on it and be my friend.'

Bekki rolled her eyes, forgetting that no-one could see her. 'I'm already your friend, dumbo.'

'No, no, that's what it's called. It's a bit like MySpace but you get to select who you talk to and who sees what. Then you can put photos up on your page and let people know what you're up to.' Jane's enthusiasm was evident.

'What if I don't want people to see what I'm up to?'

'Then you can *un*friend them. I've already had to do it to several ex-boyfriends and that girl with the wart in Miss Dillon's class. It's really easy and loads of people you know are on it already. Do you remember Kelvin Prosser who was in your year at school? All the girls fancied him.'

'How could I forget?'

'Well, I poked him on Facebook yesterday and he threw a sheep at me, it's absolutely awesome.'

'Sounds painful.'

Bekki's enthusiasm wasn't even in the same country as Jane's, but she let her sister waffle on about this brand-new phenomenon that was social media. Eventually, she was persuaded to sign up. She found many old schoolfriends on the network, and some found her, including a few that she didn't want to. In no time at all, Bekki really wished most of them hadn't. Also, in no time at all, she developed a mild addiction to status updating, poking friends and extended family members, and a very strong addiction to an interactive game called *Farmville* for several months before going cold turkey, removing the game from her Facebook account, and thus leaving several fields of virtual strawberries and potatoes to rot in the darkest recesses of the internet. Withdrawal was assisted by the arrival of even greater online distractions.

Twitter appeared a year after Facebook in two-thousand-and-six. It was a completely new kind of social media that challenged users to say anything they liked to anyone they chose using a limited number of characters and to hell with the consequences. Within six months of its global launch, Bekki was tweeting away with the rest of the internet cuckoos. It was as if Farmville had never existed.

Between two-thousand-and-five and two-thousand-and-seven, and with the exception of a couple of to do lists and reminders of important dates, Notebook Number Five contained only one other entry and response. It was time for the second one:

Dear Alice,

I think I've found a new opportunity to get all my thoughts and questions out to the world in a much bigger way in the hope that I can find more answers and eventually do more good. It's called 'social networking.' Who knows? I might even connect with like-minded people that I can meet up with. The whole planet is on there. I only have the people of Stowmarket and the surrounding areas to make a difference to.

I get so sick of all the deception and fakery in the

world and, no matter how much I try to understand it and be a better person, I'm never sure that it makes any real difference. I need people that I can talk to. This new technology is a chance for human beings to communicate with others around the world in a much more open way without any of the lies and scams. Wouldn't that be great?

Bekki xxx

A response came almost immediately.

Ah, Bekki,

Yes, the internet would be great without the lies and the fakery. Let's hope your confidence is not misplaced.

Alice.

Alice's response makes much more sense twenty years later.

Often in an important journey a person will find themselves taking two steps forwards and one step back. Bekki's social media experiment might have been a step backwards, but she was still on her way to where she wanted to be. It was a learning experience.

At first, Bekki's posts came from the place inside her that was asking all those big questions of the universe that she'd had from childhood. A couple of people, here and there, made attempts to respond with varying degrees of success. Unfortunately, they were mostly the views of those who had never been asked the question before but wanted everyone to know that they had an opinion.

Perhaps they just needed to be listened to. Perhaps they were just arseholes. Well, some of them definitely were. Others ignored it or just hit the 'like' button because they didn't know what to say but still wanted to be friends. A couple of sheep were thrown in her direction, a pastime now lost to the users of Facebook, thank goodness. Who the hell came up with that idea in the first place?

A year of attempting to communicate her deepest thoughts with the human race through Facebook hadn't got her anywhere. She kept her page, though. It was a good way of keeping an eye on her little sister and her raucous goings on. It was also very useful to be reminded to send a cake-adorned birthday message to acquaintances that didn't quite warrant a card in the post. It's nice to be nice.

Unleashing profound thoughts on Twitter proved even less fruitful. This particular social media platform, as Bekki soon discovered, was where the trolls all lived - faceless, sad people whose only pleasure in life was telling total strangers, in full view of the rest of the world, how stupid, fat, disgusting, or deserving of death they were. Sometimes they were even nastier than that.

It was a valiant attempt by Bekki to speak to the world about her ideas, her struggles and her dreams. But hardly anything came back. Nobody was sending her letters that she could stick in her notebooks. She missed speaking to Alice and Rea.

Carrie Fisher was right. The truth is everywhere, even on the internet, but it sits next to a million lies. It occurred to Bekki that social media was no different. Any truth there sat next to a billion lies, some with flying sheep. The introduction of even more ways to hide the truth were still to come with the advent of yet slicker, quicker social media platforms, invented to keep up with what the younger generation believed to be human communication.

On New Year's Eve two-thousand-and-seven, Bekki spent the day alone. It was her choice. That morning she'd checked Facebook to see where her best friends were going to be and sent them messages wishing them a Happy New Year. Some of them were choosing to spend the evening behind their online profiles. It struck Bekki as ironic that so many people were more alone than ever since they'd become connected on the world-wide web. There was no longer the need to be in the same room as your best friend to find out what they'd just had for dinner. You simply needed to check their status update. It was like you were right there with them… except that you weren't.

After three years' away in the virtual world, Bekki sat down to write a letter in Notebook Number Five.

Dear Alice and Rea,

I've missed you. I've been away for a long time, exploring the big, wide world. And then I remembered that I've hardly explored myself. I had to go away to come back and find that out. I've switched my laptop off tonight. I hope you're still there.

Happy New Year,
Bekki xxxx

Before the ink of the last 'x' was dry, a whoosh of fireworks exploded from the beer garden of the Hoof &

Handcart up the road. It was midnight. The herald of a new year and a letter from old friends.

Dear Bekki,

    We are always here. We never went away.
    Happy New Year. There is much to look forward
to.
    Alice and Rea and Rebecca too
    xxx

Chapter 19

Dear Everybody,

Ruby died yesterday. It was a heart attack. It was sudden and hopefully painless, just the way that most of us would wish to go if we could choose. She was also in her favourite place - behind the counter of her beloved café. One minute she was chatting to one of the young mums from the new Breakfast Club, the next she had slumped to the floor.

Alf dropped whatever he was doing in the kitchen and ran to Ruby's side. I've never seen him move so fast. I was clearing the table near the front door when I heard the crash. I must have only been five strides away, but by the time I got behind the counter, Alf was kneeling on the floor, cradling Ruby's head in his hands as gently as if it were a new-born kitten. 'Call an ambulance,' he said, but I hardly heard him. I don't think I moved, just stared down at the shocking scene, not knowing what to do. Luckily, Alf was not so frozen. He said it again, calmly but more firmly. 'Call an ambulance, now.'

One of the Breakfast Club mums had done some first aid training with the St John's Ambulance, and she sprang into action while I dialled 999. I think her name is Shelley, but I can't remember now. Perhaps I should have asked but my mind was racing. She tried, as best she could, to revive Ruby, pumping her chest with her hands and breathing into her mouth. All the time, Alf held Ruby's hand in his, stroking it softly and saying nothing.

By the time the paramedics came, Ruby was gone. They said it was probably a massive heart attack and she would have died instantly. There was nothing that they or anyone else could have done to save her. I think Shelley was relieved to hear them say this. I'm pretty sure that is her name.

This is all big news, I know, but it's not the only reason for writing to you all. There was a moment between Shelley pausing the first aid and the ambulance arriving that I really want to record because I don't want to forget it. Thinking about it now, I probably never will forget it, but just in case I do, I'm putting it down safely in my notebook.

Ruby's eyes were still open while that young mum was doing her first aid thing. When she stopped, out of breath and looking helpless, Alf said, 'Look at Ruby's eyes now. Look carefully.' I didn't know if he was talking to me or to the whole café. The other mums from the Breakfast Club plus an older couple from out of town were all still in the café, gathered around the counter, obviously concerned at what was happening, but Alf was looking straight at me when he said it, so I took it. I didn't want to look at

Ruby lying there like that. I was scared and upset and just wanted her to sit up and say, 'Phew! I think I passed out for a mo. Did anything happen while I was down there?' But I knew that she wasn't going to say anything ever again. Alf pressed me. 'Look, Bekki. Look at Ruby's eyes now.'

I tore my eyes away from the ceiling, where I think I must have been looking while I prayed unconsciously to some invisible deity or other, like we all do in times of crisis. Why do we always think they're on the ceiling? Then I looked straight at Ruby's face. 'I see her,' I said to Alf, and I think that's when I must have started to cry.

'No, you don't see her,' said Alf. 'That's just it. She's not there. Look again. Try to see.'

And I did look again, right into Ruby's deep brown eyes. I looked and I understood. Alf was right. She wasn't there. Her body, her face, her eyes were there, sitting motionless in their sockets, but Ruby clearly and most definitely wasn't. I couldn't speak. I just nodded my agreement to Alf and he nodded back, a slow, knowing kind of nod.

This is the thing that I want to remember. I've never seen a dead person before. On TV and in the movies, it's very different. I know that's a stupid thing to say because it's just actors pretending to be dead. But in real life - or rather in real death - there's a total absence of the person. What animates us, what makes our eyes shine, what causes us to move and speak and think and laugh, that isn't our heart or brain or face or hands because all of those things *were still there, lying on the floor. But Ruby wasn't there. She was gone.*

For the first time in my life I understood that this body that I walk around in is just a space suit that's been designed, evolved, grown in order for us to live on this planet and breath the air and eat the food, and everything else that our bodies do. It's not me. I just live inside it. When the space suit becomes uninhabitable, I will go somewhere else.

Where will I go? Where did Ruby go? That's for another day. Another massive thing to write to you about, just as big and important as letting you know about Ruby passing on. And I've decided that that's what I'll call it from now on. Her body is dead, sure, but Ruby isn't. She's 'passed on' to somewhere else. That's what my grandfather used to call it when someone died, and he was right. You don't have to be religious to see it. You don't even have to believe in anything. The fact is, once your space suit dies you are no longer inside it. It's instantaneous.

Alf didn't close the café once the ambulance crew had left. He kept it open all day but put a hand-written sign up on the door. It said, 'Dear customers: Ruby's heart stopped beating this morning. For the next three days, all teas and coffees will be free of charge. It's what she would have wanted. Funeral details to follow soon.'

The café filled up with people that afternoon, and again today, as word spread of Ruby's passing. And then a strange phenomenon happened. Almost every customer who came in to pay their respects wanted to pay full price for their drinks too. They didn't want them for free, even when we pointed out the sign on the door. Not only that, but lots of people wanted to leave a bit extra. Nobody really specified who or what they wanted the money to go towards, but people insisted that me and Alf take the money from them, even people that we knew probably couldn't afford it. In the end, Alf put a large, empty coffee jar on the counter and told people he would use the donations to feed the homeless of Stowmarket because it would carry on Ruby's work with the soup kitchen. For the first time I can remember, Alf admitted that he had made a mistake. 'I was wrong,' he said. 'This is what she would have wanted.'

By the end of the day, the coffee jar was filled with more notes than coins. I guess the customers wanted to express the value they had for Ruby. These days, perhaps the only thing people equate with the word 'value' is money. It's an unconscious reaction. That's the bloody advertising industry at work.

Tomorrow is the third day of free tea and coffee at the café. Nobody has taken one yet. It's been busier than I've ever known it, and I've been here for seven years now. Alf has barely said anything to me since Ruby's body was taken away. I know he wants to. Perhaps he's waiting for things in the café to quieten down. Tomorrow is also my day off. It will be quiet in the cottage, so I'm going to use the day to think about all of this. What I really want to know is: where did Ruby go? Maybe Alf can tell me. He's a wise old bird when he wants to be.

Keep this safe until I know some more.
Thank you.
Bekki.

And this was how Notebook Number Six began. Ruby died on the twenty third of June, two-thousand-and-eight. The number one single in the UK charts that day was *Viva La Vida* by Coldplay. It means 'Live your life'. It was a beautiful coincidence that wasn't lost on Bekki.

The whole experience was a profound one. It would be for anyone. What Bekki needed now was a deeper understanding of something that is guaranteed for all, but accepted by very few. Worse than that, it's ignored by most in the hope that it will go away. It won't.

A brief note followed soon after. There are very few letters in any of the notebooks from her. This was the first one.

Dear Bekki,
I really want to know the answer to these questions too. Please let me know when you find out.
Lots of love,
Rebecca xx

Monday was Bekki's next working day. It was always the quietest day of the week in the café. Her shift started at twelve-thirty and, for once, she was half an hour early. Outside it was pale grey and drizzling with summer rain. The question that she was burning to ask Alf was bubbling up from her stomach and into her chest as she walked in through the café door. There were no customers inside, which was fortunate. Alf was sweeping up around the counter when Bekki came in. The question erupted out of her mouth a split second later. It wasn't at all as she'd practised it in the car. 'Alf, I need to know. Where did Ruby go?' she demanded.

'Morning, Bekki.' Alf carried on sweeping as he spoke. 'Lock the door, girl.'

This calm instruction confused Bekki but also had the effect of dampening any further explosions of the verbal kind. Instead, she asked a perfectly reasonable question: 'It's lunchtime, Alf. You can't close the café at lunchtime.'

'I can do what I like,' said Alf. 'Now, lock the door, pour us a coffee and we can talk.'

Bekki did as she was told, and Alf did as he promised. He rested the broom on the corner of the counter, turned the 'Open' sign on the door to 'Closed' and they talked. It took more than one coffee. They talked for a long time.

Chapter 20

As it turned out, Alf really could do what he liked in the café now. Ruby had left it to him in her will, along with the flat upstairs. She had also left instructions that she didn't want any flowers at her funeral. Instead, people were to bring vegetables that could be made into soup for the homeless of the town on the same day.

The details of Ruby's last wishes came at the very end of the long conversation that Bekki had with Alf on that rainy Monday afternoon in June two-thousand-and-eight. The beginning of the conversation went like this:

'Come on then, girl,' said Alf. 'What's bothering you?'

'I want to know where Ruby is.' Bekki didn't know how else to phrase the question so she just came out with it.

'You know where she is,' said Alf. 'Pollard and Flitwick's Funeral Parlour.'

'You know what I mean. You told me to look at her, and I did. Her body was there and she wasn't. You wanted me to see it, and I did.'

'That's right. Did you lock the door properly?'

'Yes.'

Alf took a battered old brass tin and a Zippo lighter from his pocket, pulled out a pack of liquorice papers and some tobacco and rolled himself a skinny cigarette. 'Fetch us a saucer from the kitchen, will you?'

It was his place now. Alf could smoke indoors if he liked and neither Ruby nor anyone else could stop him. He lit his cigarette, gave a short, wheezy cough, and blew out a plume of fresh smoke. It had been eight years since Bekki had smoked a cigarette, and she wanted one now more than she had done in all that time. Alf felt her eyes on the thin brown tube between his fingers. He pushed the open tobacco tin towards Bekki. She took it with thanks and rolled a neat cigarette for herself. Her fingers hadn't forgotten how to do it.

'You're one of *them*, aren't you?' said Alf, peering at Bekki through half-closed lids.

'One of who?' said Bekki, a little light-headed from her first puff of smoke. She wasn't used to the liquorice papers either. It was a strange mix of sweet and bitter,

'One of *them*,' repeated Alf. 'A searcher. A seeker. A quester after truth. I'm one of them myself. Takes one to know one.'

'Don't you have to be holy or rich or highly intelligent to be a searcher? I'm none of those things.'

'That's a myth. All you have to be is an extraordinary ordinary person. They're harder to spot.'

'I don't know about that,' shrugged Bekki. 'Isn't everyone searching for something?'

Alf shook his head. 'Not anything beyond the essentials - eating, holidays, paying the bills. Most people, anyway. It's not their fault. We all start out asking what it's all about, but they soon knock that out of you at school, so called. That's why I dropped out when I was twelve.'

'You left school at twelve years old?'

'I didn't leave, I just dropped out. My father would

216

have whipped me senseless if he caught me playing hooky. I went to school and sat in the chair, but I wasn't going to let them un-educate me any longer. The teachers can't help it. There are some good ones, they've just got quotas to fill, haven't they?'

'But you know lots of things,' said Bekki. 'Ruby once told me that you were the wisest man she'd ever met, but she made me promise not to tell you that she'd said it.'

Alf let out a roaring laugh through a cloud of smoke. 'There you are then,' he said. 'It worked. I have been successfully un-educated by the system. Not a certificate to my name.'

'Can I talk to you about it, then?' pressed Bekki.

'Shoot.' Alf took a swig of coffee, stubbed out his cigarette in the saucer, and sat back in his chair.

Bekki took a deep breath. 'I want to know what happens to us when we die.'

'Why?'

If that was how Alf was going to play it, Bekki would have to be patient and honest. The latter would be much easier than the former. Alf was not a man to give up his hard-won wisdoms easily, and he certainly wouldn't tolerate bullshit. Bekki tried her best to gather her responses up into neater sentences. 'I want to know because I'm thirty-six years old and it's about time I started to think about it. I'm going to die some day, and I have no idea what that really means. I don't know what it means to be alive either. Shouldn't I have figured it out by now? I've had thirty-six years.'

'Ha! You're still a youngster, my girl. You wait till you're my age. That's when it really starts snapping at your heels and swelling up your joints. And don't even get me going on me prostate!'

Bekki's patience didn't stick around as long as she'd hoped. 'Dammit, Alf! I know why Ruby used to get so frustrated with you. I thought I could talk to you about these things, but you're just making fun of me like everybody else.'

A whole heap of backed-up words then poured out of Bekki's mouth. It took her by surprise. She told Alf all about the epiphany in the garden of the holiday cottage eight years before; she told him about the conversations she'd tried to have with friends and family but found no-one she could really talk to; she told him about her brother and her sister and the psychic in Kilburn; she told him how she missed her old friends who hardly came to visit and how hard it was to make new ones; she told him how she was lost; she told him how she just wanted to know the meaning of life without having to go to some monastery up a mountain and give up chocolate; she told him how much she missed Ruby. And she also told him about the notebooks.

While Bekki blurted out everything at machine gun speed through moist eyes, Alf rolled two more skinny cigarettes and passed one across the table to Bekki. 'Have you finished?' he asked. Bekki nodded and took the cigarette. 'Good. Now, go and make us both another coffee and then we can talk properly, if you'll let me get a word in.'

Bekki gathered up the empty cups and went behind the counter to make two coffees. It gave her time to wipe her eyes and take a breath. She suddenly felt empty, which meant that there was space for something else; perhaps for new understandings to get into her. Alf knew what was going on. He was indeed a wise old boy.

They talked for another hour or more. It was the first of many deep conversations between the unlikely friends. All the other discussions took place outside of café opening hours. Alf still had to make a living, and Bekki certainly needed her wages paid. She didn't go back to being a smoker full-time like before, but Alf would always share a bit of his tobacco during their long talks.

It was a few more days before Bekki wrote again in Notebook Number Six. Not in the form of a letter this time, but the faithful recording of a work in progress that would take the rest of her life to complete. There would be more of these throughout this and the next notebook. She wrote the first one the day after Ruby's funeral. There was no response from Alice, Rea or Rebecca. There was no need. Bekki was writing it with all of them.

*****

ON DEATH AND LIVING by Bekki Reeves

It will seem incredible to people in the future, and definitely to those in the ancient past, to discover that many humans living in the twenty first century understood nothing about death and dying. Today, in many parts of the Western world at least, it is even considered a taboo subject. Death has come to everyone who's ever lived on Earth, and will come to everyone who is alive right now, but while we celebrate birth, we refuse to look into the face of death until it becomes inevitable. Why?

The only answer I have come to so far is this: to be alive must be so important and so hard won that none of us want it to end. Even if a person believes in an afterlife or reincarnation or any variation of existence after death, the only people who invite death upon themselves before their time are those who are very sick, either physically or mentally.

Personally, I haven't yet made up my mind about whether or not there is life after death. That needs a lot more time and thought to be true for me. If I believe in anything to do with mortality right now, it's that what happens to a person is probably what they believe will happen most strongly. The power of the mind is an extraordinary thing. That's why placebos work. If a person strongly believes that their existence will continue in a different form somewhere else in the universe, or in their own definition of heaven or hell, then I reckon that's where they'll go. If a person believes they become nothing but worm food or ashes on the ground to be recycled into the planet, then I reckon that's where they'll go, because that must be what they want.

I know what I want. I want to exist somewhere else in the universe after I leave this place. I want to go somewhere that I can't even begin to imagine, in some other kind of body or state that I can explore with. But then I've always been an inquisitive kind of person, and I'm really hoping it's possible to still ask questions after I die. It would be so sad if I couldn't. I might even find answers that don't exist here.

One thing I do know for certain. When a person passes away, it's absolutely evident to see that they were never their physical body, because that definitely stays right here on earth. But whatever it was that caused the animation of that body, or the light in those eyes, it disappears in an instant. I've seen it. Not only that, the empty body starts to rot as soon as the person leaves and their heart stops beating. Life has left the building.

So, if life is such a vital, powerfully strong urge in everything that lives - because no animal wants to die either - do we give it the importance and the reverence that it deserves? I know that for most of my life I haven't thought about it like that. I guess I just thought that living was just breathing and moving around and not being dead.

How do we change all this in ourselves? How do we become a bit more conscious? I only have a simple answer. We live. Not only that, we live like we mean it.

5th July 2008.

Chapter 21

Between seven and ten years is supposedly the length of time on average that it takes the human body to replace all of its cells. This is according to multiple sites on the internet, so it must be true. If it is true, it means that each of us has the potential to be an entirely different person every seven years... unless we teach the new cells, including those in our brains, to follow our old habits and inclinations and produce the same old stuff as always.

It was now two-thousand-and-ten, two years since Alf had inherited the café from Ruby, and seven years since Jake had knocked on the door of Bekki's cottage out of the blue. She'd followed his career on social media in all that time. Initially, she checked on his whereabouts almost to the level of stalker, but more recently she would just check out his status updates once in a while, sending birthday and Christmas messages with silly emojis attached. He would repay the favour and remember to comment on her important days, and both were just pleased to be connected to each other's lives, even in a virtual way. It seemed that Jake had made the most of all that cell renewal. Those seven years had changed him, and Bekki was about to find that out.

It was a Thursday afternoon in October and unseasonably warm. Even the tables on the pavement outside the café were full and the coffee machine was puffing hard. Alf was forced to come out of the kitchen and greet the customers at the counter. Luckily, most of those inside were regulars and so used to his particular brand of customer service.

Bekki was serving a couple of builders at a table near the toilets when Jake walked in. She was concentrating on keeping the tray in her hands level as, despite his apparent lack of generosity, Alf always filled the mugs up to the brim. Bekki was just lifting the first steaming coffee mug off the tray when a familiar voice spoke over her shoulder.

'Hi Bekki. How are you doing?'

It would be an understatement to say that Jake's unmistakable tones surprised Bekki down to her fingertips. She whirled round, still holding the mug, and a hot, brown splash of coffee flew out of it and covered the builder's lap underneath it with a dark, steaming stain. The man let out a high-pitched expletive, causing Bekki to drop the tray onto the table with a clatter, inviting a 'Hooray' from the other customers. Bekki tried to ignore them as she desperately started to wipe the lap of the now delighted builder with the front of her apron. 'Oh, jeez, I'm so sorry. I'll get you another coffee on the house. Sorry, sorry,' wipe, wipe.

'Don't worry about it, love,' said the builder. 'That's what overalls are for,' and he sat back and put out his arms to allow Bekki's apron greater access to his crotch.

'Lucky bastard,' said the other builder.

Bekki picked up the tray and mopped what she could on the table with her now sopping wet apron. 'I'll be back in a minute. Sorry.' She hurried back towards the counter and motioned with her head for Jake to follow. 'What are you doing here?' she asked him over her shoulder.

'I was just in the neighbourhood and thought I'd drop by. It's good to see you.'

Alf had been watching all this from behind the counter and had already set the machine going for the replacement coffees. 'Well done, girl,' he said with a smirk. 'You've just made a hairy-arsed builder's day. Who's this, then?' he asked, pointing his thumb at Jake.

'Oh, this is Jake, my...erm...' stuttered Bekki, still in shock.

'Her ex-boyfriend,' said Jake, trying to help.

'Ah, the musician guy.' Alf was being unusually convivial, which just added to Bekki's bewilderment. 'You're a bass player, right?'

'That's right,' said Jake who was always convivial.

'We should get together some time and form a rhythm section,' said Alf, putting the last bit of froth on the replacement coffees. 'I play the bongos myself.'

'Cool,' said Jake.

'When did you ever play the bongos?' asked Bekki.

'There's lots of things about me you don't know.' Alf put the coffees on a clean tray and slid it over the counter to Bekki. 'Take these over to Laurel and Hardy over there, then make you and your friend a couple of drinks and take your break. One of the tables outside has just come free.'

'Are you sure you can manage?' said Bekki. She wasn't quite prepared for a face-to-face coffee date with Jake.

'If I can't manage I'll kick everyone out on their arses and close the place. Now, get your drinks and then get out of my sight for half an hour. I don't want word to spread among the building trade that there's lap dancing available for the price of a coffee.'

'But, I didn't...'

'Now!' Alf flicked a tea towel over his shoulder and put his hands on his hips. This always meant he was serious. He turned to Jake and smiled showing all of the yellowing, nicotine-stained teeth he still had left. 'If I were you, young man, I'd go and grab that outside table before somebody else does. And go easy on her. Looks like you took her by surprise.'

Jake smiled back and gave a little salute to Alf, which the old boy enjoyed immensely. Then he dutifully went outside and took a seat at the empty table on the pavement in full view of everyone inside. Bekki followed a couple of minutes later with a cappuccino for herself and a latté for Jake. That used to be his coffee shop drink of choice. She hoped it still was.

The sun was strong for October, and its brightness was bouncing off the white metal table, throwing a glow across Jake's face. He hadn't aged a bit. Probably all those brand-new skin cells. 'It's good to see you,' he said again, once Bekki had settled herself in front of him. 'Have you found yourself yet?'

'What do you mean?' said Bekki. She wasn't expecting that kind of question so early in the conversation.

'Your old mates told me that you left London and your job and everything so that you could go on a spiritual journey to find yourself.'

'When did you see my mates?'

'Oh, you know, they've been to some of my gigs and

stuff. I always ask after you. And I see your status updates on Facebook.'

'That's nice.' In reality, Bekki thought this was much more than nice. She had been surprised at how much she'd missed this guy. She'd kept herself deliberately single since moving to Suffolk. Questions of existence had taken up most of her weekends. It had been a long time. With Jake sitting in front of her, the good memories and the best times were flooding back and she suddenly felt that perhaps single wasn't the way to go anymore. Nostalgia is like that. It only brings back the good bits.

'I always thought spiritual journeys took people to places like India and Bali, not Stowmarket.' Jake wasn't being sarcastic. It wasn't in his repertoire.

'A journey of self-development doesn't take you to a place on a map. It takes you to a place inside yourself. That part goes with you no matter how far you travel.' Bekki lifted the coffee cup to her lips to stop herself saying any more for the moment. The words coming out of her mouth sounded all high and mighty when spoken out loud. After all, she was speaking to the best zombie killer in Finchley, or at least that's what he was all those years ago. He probably wouldn't be interested in Bekki's coffee shop philosophising.

'Hmmm,' said Jake, then he paused for what seemed to Bekki like hours and took a swig from his own coffee cup. The conversation had become a little awkward. Jake finally broke the tension with more tension. 'Is that why you finished with me?'

'What?' Always a useful word when attempting to buy some time.

'You never really explained exactly why you left me, and I guess I've always wanted to know. I was going to ask you when you came to that gig in Ipswich, but you left before I had a chance. Maybe I could ask now.'

'That's fair, I suppose.' Bekki took another sip of coffee and remembered something that she herself had written in one of the notebooks the last time she saw Jake. While she was busy trying to change herself, she'd forgotten that time had moved on for everyone else in the world too. The man sitting before her was not the lad that she'd walked out on ten years before. And she was not the same girl either. 'I'm sorry,' said Bekki. 'Everything in the world seemed like a lie at the time, and that's all I could see. I had to get away to find anything I could that was true.'

A look of puzzlement fell upon Jake's face. There were lines on his forehead that weren't there ten years ago. He was forty-two now. That's what happens. 'I don't think I ever lied to you,' said Jake.

'I know. It wasn't you.'

'Yeah, yeah, I know. It's not you, it's me.'

'But it really is. Or, it was.' Bekki reached across and took Jake's hand in hers across the table. He didn't pull away. 'I didn't think you'd understand. We never talked about anything deep, so I thought it was best to do this alone. That wasn't your fault. It's not an easy journey. Half the time I have no idea what I'm doing.'

Jake squeezed Bekki's hand gently. 'I can help with that.'

'How?'

'Easy. I don't know what I'm doing *all* of the time.' Jake took a gulp from his mug and smiled. 'Do you remember my mate Whiskers who worked in the Horse & Rucksack?'

Bekki wasn't sure where this was going but was pleased at the diversion. 'Ummm… yes.'

'Do you know how he got his nickname?'

'I guess it's that pointy goatee of his.'

'Nope. It's because when he was seven years old he ate a spoonful of cat food for a dare. He did it once and he's been called Whiskers ever since.'

'What's your point?'

'He's forty-five years old and still being labelled with something he did when he was seven.'

'That's funny,' said Bekki.

'Yeah, but it's kind of sad too. People change, you know.'

Bekki looked at the man sat in front of her as if she'd never looked at him before and nodded. The two old lovers laughed and drank coffee in the autumn sunshine. Bekki told Jake all about Ruby and the notebooks and her clumsy search for the meaning of life. Jake told her about Breadroll Caravan and how the band had split last month when the singer started going out with some reality TV star and they got offered their own Channel 5 show for an undisclosed sum and a lifetime's supply of fake tan. Now he was wondering what to do with the next part of his life.

'I've missed you, Bekks,' said Jake. 'We had fun.'

'I've missed you too,' said Bekki. 'How long are you in Suffolk for?'

'As long as I like.'

'Where are you staying?'

Jake shrugged. 'Any decent hotels in Stowmarket?'

Bekki couldn't honestly think of one that had ever

been recommended by a customer. 'You can stay with me, if you like. I've got a spare room.'

The café door opened then and Alf stuck his head outside. 'I've got a spare room upstairs, if you want to stay here, lad.'

'How the hell did you hear us from inside?' said Bekki.

'Your body language is very loud,' said Alf. 'Break over. Back on your head, girl.'

Jake did stay at Bekki's that night. And the next night, and the next week. His share of the band's publishing royalties was rather healthy and meant that he didn't have to rush to make any decisions. That's the most useful thing that money provides - time.

Two months later, Jake was helping out in the kitchen of the café three days a week. As it turned out, he was a natural chef despite never having poached an egg in his life. Not all talents are revealed at once. It was almost Christmas and he was turning out turkey platters and chocolate yule logs like a long-lost Hairy Biker.

The café shut the day before Christmas Eve for a fortnight's holiday. Alf turned the 'Open' sign to 'Closed' and asked Bekki and Jake to sit down at the table near the counter for a quick chat before going home. The old boy disappeared into the kitchen and came back shortly with a bottle of brandy and three glasses. He poured them one each and they raised a toast to the café, to Ruby and to the future.

'I want to talk to you about something,' said Alf. 'It's important so you'd better listen up.'

'Sounds ominous,' said Bekki. 'You're not getting rid of us, are you?' She was only half joking.

'It's the other way around,' said Alf. 'You're getting rid of me.'

'I could never do that, ever,' said Bekki, concern now showing on her face. 'This is your home as well as your café.'

'Of course you couldn't. What are you talking about?' said Alf.

'I think Bekki's trying to figure out what *you're* talking about,' said Jake.

'I'm going away for a bit,' said Alf.

'Where?' said Bekki and Jake together.

'Manitoba.'

'Manitoba?' said Bekki. 'Isn't that a kind of sea mammal?'

'No,' said Jake. 'It's in Canada.

'How do you know?' said Bekki.

'We did a gig there a few years back. A club called The Angry Beaver. It was a good night. Bit cold.'

'What's in Manitoba?' asked Bekki.

'Ancestors,' said Alf. 'I've been doing some research on the computer at the library. My great grandfather was from the Cree tribe and some cousins have invited me over. They said I could stay as long as I like, which at my age might not be too long.'

Bekki sat back in her chair astonished. 'You're part Native American? That's amazing.'

'They don't call it that nowadays. It's First Nation Peoples.'

'Cool,' said Jake.

'Wow!' said Bekki.

'How old are you?' asked Jake.

'None of your business,' replied Alf.

'When are you going?' said Bekki.

'Boxing Day.'

'What?!' exclaimed Bekki. 'You can't.'

'Yes, I can,' said Alf. 'I can do what I like. It's my café, you said so yourself.'

'How will we manage?' said Bekki.

'Well, I must admit, I was worried about that myself until young fella-me-lad here turned up. But I think you make a good team. I can trust you not to do anything stupid now.'

That was the nicest thing Alf had ever said to Bekki. It caused an involuntary tear to well up in her eye and drop onto her cheek. Jake saw it and put his arm around her shoulder. Alf saw it and ignored it.

'Drink up,' said Alf. 'I'll pour us another.'

The old man managed to pack everything he needed for his adventure into a green canvas army kit bag. He liked to travel light. Bekki and Jake drove him to the airport on Boxing Day and waved him goodbye until he disappeared into a sea of pasty-skinned holiday makers desperately making their way to anywhere that had deck chairs, sangria, and sunshine.

It was quiet in the car on the way back to Bluebell Cottage. The café would be closed for another ten days. That would give Bekki time to adjust. Alf would be gone for a while. He was an old man. He might be gone forever. Everything was changing again and Bekki was being presented with a future that she hadn't planned for. Had she learned anything at all in the last ten years or was it all just intellectual scribblings in a notebook? Here was an opportunity now to put all these grand ideas about honesty and integrity and humanity into practise in front of real people and a steaming coffee machine. She began to have ideas. She was scared and a little overwhelmed, but she definitely began to have ideas. Bekki glanced at Jake in the passenger seat and smiled. She was grateful not to be alone.

The spare bedroom at Bluebell Cottage had been turned into a makeshift music room for Jake. He had moved into Bekki's bedroom. It happened quite quickly and naturally. At three o'clock in the morning, on the day that Alf left, Bekki was wide awake. She left Jake sleeping soundly and went downstairs to find Notebook Number Six on the white bookcase. She switched on the lamp next to the sofa and settled down to write.

Dear Alice and Rea,

I'm about to enter a new time, and it is like a blank page. I have a space that is the café, where I can create something good in the world, even if it's just a small part of the world.

I want to be able to reach people and talk to them, just in case it makes a difference. I don't know how yet, but it feels like the right time. I'll carry on with Ruby's soup kitchen, if I can find some help with that, but I want to do more. I want to keep learning and pass on what I learn, if it's of any use to anyone. Ruby used to say that if you can make one person's life a little bit better every day, then you've changed the world. I asked her how she did that. She said she smiled at them.

I'm not a teacher or a doctor or anything, but
I can smile at strangers. That's a start. I'll let you
know how I get on.
   Bekki xxx

Rea answered on behalf of herself and Alice. It was a
simple response.

Dear Bekki,
   Ruby was right.
   Rea x

And that was the final entry in Notebook Number
Six. Bekki went back upstairs to bed. Jake was still asleep.
Nights were always so silent outside Bluebell Cottage.
There was time over Christmas while the café was closed
to rest and gather their strength for what was to come.

Chapter 22

It is the present day. Much has happened in the world since that last entry in Notebook Number Six, and much had happened in the lives of Bekki and Jake and the customers of Tiffin Teas. Notebook Number Seven documented the most important events of the intervening years, and the big questions that had been asked in the previous notebooks gave way to deeper understandings on the state of the human race and ideas on how to stay intact in the face of it all. In between the big stuff, Bekki also catalogued the goings on in the Reeves family.

Jane was now an 'influencer' on social media with two million followers and counting. She specialised in humorous grooming tips for the over forties, accompanied by popular dance tracks from the eighties and much advertising revenue. She was a natural, and had even appeared as a contestant on a popular ITV quiz show. She came last in a quite spectacular way and gained several thousand more followers as a result.

Mr and Mrs Reeves were now retired and living in a bungalow in the Suffolk seaside town of Felixstowe. Relations between Bekki and her mother had become softer over the years, as these things mellow with age. However, Felixstowe was just far enough away from Bluebell Cottage to keep visits down to one a month. In any case, Pamela Reeves had joined the local W.I. and found them remarkably open-minded. She was currently head of the nude swimming committee.

Bekki's younger brother, Jimmy, did finally get to run a bar. Not in Brighton, but near his parents in Felixstowe. Jane had bought it with the proceeds from an immensely popular online campaign about waxing after the menopause. Jimmy's natural exuberance meant that the local community embraced him with ease. He's now one of the organisers of the annual Pride celebrations in the town. Last year, Mrs Reeves won second prize in the costume category. She went as Sylvester Stallone's mother.

In the year twenty-twelve, there had been an Olympic Games in London that millions had complained about until it happened, and then everybody loved it. Bekki installed a TV in the café for the duration, and the place was busier than ever. Even the Paralympics had the nation gripped for the first time and people queued for tickets for every event.

Instagram was born in the same year. Smart phones became the norm and people started walking around with their heads down, endeavouring to communicate without actually speaking, and forgetting how to spell without predictive text. Bekki wished that Alf had been at the café then. He would have banned mobile phones and sod anyone who complained. She continued to receive long letters from the old man, which were so much nicer, and easier to paste into Notebook Number Seven, than emails and text messages. Alf had surprisingly beautiful handwriting.

When the voters of Britain were offered a referendum on whether or not to stay in the European Union, Bekki documented it in Notebook Number Seven too. It simply said this:

What the hell is going on?

And then she never wrote about politics again. There was no response from Rea, Alice or Rebecca under that particular entry. There would be more than enough written on social media for the rest of time, and most of it angry and insulting on all sides.

Artificial Intelligence, that staple of Science Fiction movies, became available to anyone who had a computer or a mobile phone. The inventors of the technology clearly had never seen any of these movies, because if they had, they might have thought it through a bit more carefully. Within days, possibly hours, the abuse and misuse of the technology had begun with nobody having a clue as to how to close this particular Pandora's Box. They should have asked Will Smith. Bekki wrote a brief note on this world-changing piece of software:

Isn't it interesting how the human race has adopted Artificial Intelligence so quickly? But then, I guess if you have no natural human intelligence it's useful to have a substitute. Personally, I don't trust it.

It wasn't usually Bekki's style to be so cynical, so she re-read this statement and then added a few words underneath.

'Most' of the human race, that is. Not everybody.

This satisfied her for a while. After all these years, she was still working on reducing deception, judgement, and all the other things she didn't want to be by one percent every time. Nobody's perfect, though. Sometimes you have to allow yourself a day off to rant at the world before moving on.

As the population of the world swelled to almost eight billion, climate change became a reality, the housing shortage became a housing crisis, and more and more people were turning up at the soup kitchen. By the year twenty-nineteen, there were too many people for Bekki and her small group of volunteers to cope with, and so they joined forces with a local charity and founded 'Ruby's Food Bank' to feed all kinds of people in the town and beyond twice a week.

By this time, and much to the delight of every English Teacher in Britain, the whole country finally understood what the word 'pronoun' meant. Not only that, it would be used with increasing regularity under email signatures and social media biogs across the Western World. 'Now, if only we can get them to understand the difference between 'there,' 'their' and 'they're', we'll be laughing,' said every English teacher in Britain.

Every day since Bekki had that first epiphany in the garden of the holiday cottage, a war had been going on somewhere on the planet. Total peace hadn't happened even once in all that time. Always, somewhere, there was a fight happening over a scrap of land or well full of oil or some twisted ideology. Bekki wrote about this too. It was a long piece covering several pages, but really, she summed it up to her own satisfaction in the last paragraph:

No matter how many conflicts are fought, or how many people die, the human race has still not learnt the lessons of the past. The only people that ever benefit from war are arms dealers and undertakers.

And then, in the year two-thousand-and-twenty, a new virus was discovered in China and the café had to close its doors to customers. That's when Alf returned from Canada. He moved back into the flat above the café and Bekki was more pleased to see him than she could have imagined. She and Jake formed what the government of the day called 'a bubble' with Alf, which was where two households could mix together without the need for quarantine in order to support each other as needed. This law was only applicable to the general public, however, so that the government could carry on having parties and snogging colleagues without fear of imprisonment. They were probably just letting off steam. It was a difficult time.

Donations for Ruby's Food Bank came in more than ever, despite the café and the food bank itself being closed. Then Bekki had the idea of using the ingredients and cooking up dishes that could be delivered to the most vulnerable in the town, either for free or for a donation. It would help to pay the bills until they could open. The idea was a great success, and Alf took it upon himself to make most of the deliveries on his old bicycle while wearing a rainbow face mask and a fireman's helmet. He never told anyone where he got the helmet from, but it looked new.

Bekki documented all this on social media, and for a while Alf went viral in a good way.

Millions of people across the world died as a result of the virus. For a while, the real heroes were not movie stars or footballers or heads of state, but delivery drivers and nurses and supermarket workers. But people have short memories. The simple pleasure of hearing bird song in city centres and seeing clear skies with no contrails was soon forgotten.

When the café opened its doors again, the customers found that the walls had been painted. Instead of the practical cream emulsion, they were striped in a rainbow of colour. Alf had a lot of time on his hands during lockdown and wanted to brighten the place up. The customers came back, but some of the older regulars would never return.

Mrs Sudley was one of the tragic victims of that global pandemic. Most tragic of all was that she died alone. Bekki didn't have a chance to say goodbye and thank her for being such a good neighbour. In the old lady's honour, Bekki planted a whole bed of rhubarb in the garden. She would make pies for the food bank with them one day and think of her.

Jake's old bandmate, Eric, was bequeathed the cottage next door in his grandmother's will, proving once again how small the world really is. Together they converted Mrs Sudley's large shed at the bottom of the garden into a proper music studio, soundproofed and wired for electricity via a large solar panel on the roof. From the once humble shed they went on to build a thriving music therapy business. By the end of two-thousand-and-twenty-three Jake had hardly any spare time to help in the café. It was time for Alf to put an ad in the window.

The generous soul that was Ruby gave much away while she was alive, but she rarely *threw* anything away. In the back of a drawer in the café kitchen, and much to Bekki's amazement, Alf found the original window notice that she herself had responded too all those years ago. The paper was a little yellow around the edges, but there it was:

'*VACANCY: Part-time café assistant required. Must be flexible, numerate and polite. Apply within.*'

The sign went up on a Wednesday afternoon. Only one candidate came in to the café on the following day. Her name was Meena and she lived two streets away. She'd never been in the café before. Alf interviewed her himself, insisting that he was a far better judge of character than Bekki. This was probably true.

After several pre-prepared questions over americanos, Alf shook the girls hand and held the door open for her as she left. 'That's the one,' said Alf as he walked back behind the counter to where Bekki was waiting.

'Are you sure?' asked Bekki. 'She's the only one you've interviewed so far. We've only had the sign up since yesterday.'

'She's the one,' asserted Alf. 'Now, take that sign out of the window. She starts on Monday.'

'What makes you so certain?'

'She reminds me of you,' and then Alf went out through the back of the kitchen to have another cigarette break.

Meena fitted into the café well. She was as friendly as Alf was grumpy and the customers liked her. This pleased the old man - who still refused to admit his age to anyone, although he must have been in his eighties by now - and it meant that he could spend more time in the kitchen inventing recipes and having fag breaks. Bekki had assumed Ruby's old position behind the counter and was now as adept with blue cloths as her mentor had been.

One Friday afternoon, Meena had finished her shift but didn't seem in a hurry to go home. Bekki noticed. 'Do you fancy a hot chocolate before you go home?' she asked the girl.

Meena nodded and took a seat at the table by the big window. The café was empty now and soon the 'Open' sign would be turned to 'Closed.' Bekki made them both a frothy mug of chocolate with sprinkles of nutmeg and sat down. Meena was twenty years old. Bekki was now fifty-two and carried a little extra padding between the chair and her bones. She got herself comfy and waited to see what it was that was troubling her young assistant. She didn't have to wait long.

'Can I ask you something?' said Meena.

'Sure,' said Bekki. 'I can't promise I'll have the answer, though.'

'You probably have.'

'Let's see, shall we,' and Bekki blew some froth off the top of her hot chocolate and took a sip.

'I don't know who to talk to,' said Meena, looking uncomfortable.

'Is that your question?'

'No.'

'Then let's start again.'

'Okay, I'll try.' Meena took a sip from her own mug, took a deep breath and tried her best to explain something that was impossible for her to encapsulate in one sentence. She tried, though. 'Sometimes it feels like the world is so full of lies and scams that no-one can tell what is true and what is false, and I'm worried that I'll end up behaving like everybody else and make excuses for it, but it's not natural, is it? There has to be a way of living that has some kind of purpose but I don't know where to start and I just wish that someone would rip off the mask that everything is wearing and just tell the truth.' Meena only stopped there because she'd run out of air. She took a deep breath in and slumped down into her seat.

'That was a big question,' said Bekki, and she smiled at the girl in front of her. This is what Alf meant.

'Sorry,' said Meena. I think about these things a lot, but I have no idea how to change it. Where do I start? How do you do it?'

'How do I what?'

'How do you stay sane in the face of all this? You're the most *human* person I've ever met.'

Bekki was a little taken aback by this. If she'd changed that much since the day that she herself had responded to Ruby's ad, it had been a slow process and she hadn't realised that any of her attempts could even be seen from the outside. 'It's a long journey,' she said. 'Are you sure you want to take it? Once you rip off that mask, you can't put it back.'

'I don't mind. I just want to know how to start.'

'Very well,' said Bekki. 'I'll give you some advice that I got a long time ago, that I've been trying to take on ever since.' Meena sat up a little in her chair, waiting for the revelation. 'This is what you do,' said Bekki. 'The next

243

time you feel yourself about to be critical or judgemental or deceitful towards another human being, reduce it by one percent.'

'One percent? Is that all?'

'That's a start. Then the next time, you reduce it by another one percent, and then another one and another. You won't notice the change straight away, but others will.'

'That seems too simple,' said Meena, slumping back down again.

'It does, doesn't it?' said Bekki. 'But it isn't. It takes a lot of practise and sometimes you'll fail. That doesn't matter. Just keep going. Then one day you'll discover that people will want to come and talk to you to find out what your secret is.'

'Like I did.'

'That's right. It's a very big secret I have to tell you, though. Are you sure you're ready?'

'I'm ready,' and Meena sat back up in her chair again to prove it.

'Here it is.' Bekki paused and leaned forward across the table for dramatic effect. 'Be a little kinder to others and to yourself,' then she picked up her mug of hot chocolate and went back behind the counter. 'Goodnight, Meena. Turn the sign round on your way out.'

Meena did as she was asked and went home. She wasn't working that weekend so she had two whole days to think about what Bekki said. At first, she was a little bemused and rather impatient, but then take-off and landing are the most difficult parts of any journey. On Sunday evening, she switched off her phone and her laptop, tore off a couple of pages from the magnetic shopping list pad that was hanging on the fridge, and sat on her bed to try and gather her thoughts. Typing into a device wouldn't have been any good. It would have been too easy to press delete. She didn't want to bother Bekki with all the big questions that were rattling around her brain until she could look at them herself. She wrote and thought and wrote and thought until she had to go back to the fridge to get a couple more pages and a slab of lemon drizzle cake.

On Monday morning, Meena was back at work in the café. She arrived a few minutes before the door was due to be opened to customers and went to the back of the kitchen to hang up her coat on the hooks. Bekki and Alf were already there, sitting at the small staff table by the back door, drinking their first coffees of the day and deep in conversation.

'Good morning, young lady,' said Alf. 'Good weekend?'

'It was different,' said Meena.

'Always good to be different,' said Alf.

'Am I disturbing something?'

'It's nothing secret,' said Bekki. 'We're just planning some important changes.'

'Oh,' said Meena. 'You're not closing the café, are you?'

'Quite the opposite,' said Bekki. 'It will be open even more. We're going to start comedy and music nights on Wednesdays. Alf's going to be the compere.'

'Really?'

'Yep. Turns out he has a genius for comedy.'

'I prefer satire,' said Alf. 'I'm the Peter Cook of Stowmarket.'

'Who's Peter Cook?' asked Meena.

'The ignorance of youth,' huffed Alf. 'I'm going out the

back for a fag,' and he picked up the cigarette from the table that was already rolled and nipped out the back door.

'He's going to be a star,' laughed Bekki.

'Are you sure he'll be okay? I mean, how old is he?'

'Nobody knows. In the meantime, I've got you a little gift.'

'You didn't have to do that.'

'I know. It's my one percent extra for today.' Bekki fetched a slim, rectangular package from her bag, all wrapped in brown paper, and held it out to Meena. She unwrapped it with care. Inside was a brand-new notebook with a bright blue and yellow cover, neatly ruled inside with margins.

'Thank you so much,' said Meena. 'It's just what I needed.'

Chapter 23

Notebook Number Eight is not to be found on the shelves of the white bookcase that had stood in the living room of Bluebell Cottage for all these years. It's the same old bookcase that holds the old dictionary and the volumes of facts and figures and world statistics that were hardly opened anymore. Oh, and three or four works of fiction that nobody could bear to throw away for long-forgotten reasons. And, of course, all the other notebooks. Notebook Number Eight does not belong to us anymore. It was set free into the world.

The idea came to Bekki on the evening of the day she gave Meena her gift. Jake was out running one of his music workshops and the café was closed.

There was a saying that Ruby used to love: 'If you want to have a diamond you must first give it away.' It felt like an ancient sentiment, or maybe Ruby made it up. Either way, it didn't matter. On that Monday evening, with the washing up done and the TV switched off, Ruby's saying popped into her head and Bekki wanted to do something about it immediately.

She fetched all the notebooks from the white bookcase, spread them out on the kitchen table and made a cup of coffee. As Bekki leafed through her trusty paper companions, she laughed, she cried, and occasionally winced with embarrassment. She couldn't remember writing half of the things she had so lovingly recorded at the time, but there were some little nuggets of wisdom within the pages.

Bekki spent the next few days poring over the notebooks to pick out the things that she wanted to share with others. In her best handwriting and with her favourite pen, she copied a different thought or saying or idea onto a separate page in Notebook Number Eight and then cut each page out with care. Each one would later be placed in an envelope to post, or put in a simple frame to give to someone, and one or two were even posted on her Instagram page for anyone who cared to find it, and some people did. One of the pages might be specially meant for a certain friend or relation, or another for a regular customer in the café. Some were more general and would be kept inside Notebook Number Eight until the time was right to give one away, as circumstances decreed. She gave the first one to Jake. It said:

We are all on a journey through life, and each of us must find our own path. Sometimes two paths run alongside each other with no conflict or judgement. Draw strength from this companionship because it means we're not alone. This is where love can be found... and sometimes picnics.

There are still lots of these special pages left, kept safe on the white bookcase, waiting for Bekki to set them free into the world. After all, that's what everything and everyone really wants. To be set free.

Acknowledgements

My eternal thanks go to AJ Deane for being my editor, champion, best friend, provider of caffeine as needed, and also my husband. I marvel constantly at his unwavering belief in me, which is more belief than I have in myself. I will try to live up to it in the future, and hope that he knows that I believe in him too.

And to photographer, artist, kindred spirit and old friend Andrea Kennard for being so generous with her talents and allowing me, once again, to use some of her beautiful work for the enhancement of my own.

Thank you also to the bookshops whose owners and managers liked my books enough to actually put them on their shelves between John Le Carré and Lewis Carroll: Diss Publishing Bookshop; Dial Lane Books; Stillwater Books; Halesworth Bookshop; Woodbridge Bookshop; The Script Haven; The Book Cellar; The Bookshop in Helston; The Nook in Lavenham; and the store managers at Waterstones in Bury St Edmunds, Colchester and Chelmsford. Some of these emporiums of magic even sold some copies.

My gratitude also goes out to the public libraries of Suffolk and Norfolk who stocked my books and were kind enough to let me go in and talk about what I do to innocent members of the public, especially to Halesworth Library where I am a very proud patron.

And finally, to two great exponents of literature who have both left us and will sadly write no more: My heartfelt gratitude to Fay Weldon and Benjamin Zephaniah. Both of these remarkable people took the time to help and encourage an unknown author, simply because they saw something worth encouraging and were generous enough to do it asking for nothing in return. In their own unique ways, they personally helped me in my writing journey more than they knew. I am a better writer because of it, and I will never forget them.

Jackie Carreira, Suffolk 2024